WILL SHE KILL HIM, OR SAVE HIM?

Noah is the levelheaded twin who has always looked out for Liam, not that many people could tell the difference between the two of them. Their coping mechanisms for the last decade of hell was to make jokes and laugh it all off. It has its upsides and downsides, which includes no one in the pack really taking them seriously.

When their new, resident witch offered to scry for his mate, he agreed, ready to settle down, but the last thing he expected was to find out that his mate was a raven shifter - who's people are notorious assassins within the paranormal world.

It's impossible to get in contact with a raven unless you wanted to hire them to kill someone, and no one really knows anything about them. Noah knew there was no way he'd ever find her, let alone convince her to choose him over her flock.

Then one day, out of the blue, she shows up....with a contract to kill him and his entire pack.

WOLF CLAIM

THE BLUE MOUNTAIN WOLF PACK SERIES

EMMA DEAN

WOLF CLAIM
BLUE MOUNTAIN WOLF PACK

AUTHOR'S NOTE

All of my paranormal books exist in the same universe. The more you read the more you see familiar faces. You don't need to read them in any particular order, or to know any others before starting any of my series or standalones.

<3 Emma

Join my group for the spoiler thread for each release in the series!

Emma's Enclave

P.S. See Other Books for links

Council of Paranormals Timeline

A Devil's Huntress

Alpha Wolf

Broken Wolf

Whiskey and Hellfire

Wolf Moon

Vaudeville Runaway

Wolf Curse
Wolf Bite
Wolf Claim

Spotted Her First

For Fox Sake
All Foxed Up
What the Fox

A Bandit's Prequel
To Catch a Bandit
Make Out Like Bandits

Something Wicked
Wicked Games
No Rest for the Wicked
A Wicked Raven
Wicked Blood
As Wicked As They Come
Wicked Little Things

The Wicked Will Rise
Wicked Queen

WOLF CLAIM

1

NOAH

Watching his twin with his new mate was both harder and easier than he'd anticipated. Noah couldn't believe there was really someone out there that fit his brother so perfectly despite their rocky beginning.

Zoe had been a total bitch and she still was, no doubt about that, but now she was on their side. Noah honestly hadn't expected her to treat him like he was just as important as Liam.

That was unusual for a mate, but to be fair, their situation was pretty unusual.

Wolf twins were rare, and always insanely codependent from what he'd heard through the grapevine. There was a set of born Alpha twins on the East Coast that had caused a buzz in the wolf community, but he hadn't heard much about them since they'd gone off to college.

Noah sighed and tapped his fingers on the steering wheel of the small car he preferred to drive whenever they had to be in the city. This may or may not be the right course of action considering their current situation, but it wasn't like they could just abandon all their territorial duties either.

They were lucky the Cirque de Nuit pride had stayed on a bit longer in Portland or they'd be totally fucked.

The Alpha of the Cirque de Nuit pride wouldn't interfere in a territory dispute, but they were a traveling Sanctuary, which meant they would help with pretty much anything else if it meant keeping people safe.

Liam practically ripped the door off its hinges when he opened it and grinned at Noah. "We're almost done in there. Are you sure you don't want to come take a look?"

"I'd rather choke on your cooking than go in there." Noah narrowed his eyes at the neon girl dancing around a pole and swallowed down a growl.

"Geez, dude, you don't need to be so melodramatic," Liam teased, tossing a bottle of water and a paper bag on the front seat. "Eat the sandwich so you're not such a cranky bitch. Zoe's almost done inspecting the girls with Laura. Then we'll go back to the townhouse. Hopefully Kai will have an update by then."

Hopefully, but Noah wasn't going to hold his breath. The way things were going down...well, it was a little too familiar and it was making his anxiety spike. Liam seemed too lost in his brand-new mate bond to notice, but Noah knew that was an act.

Liam was terrified he was going to lose his mate as well as this peace they had ever since Kai took over. It had been a rough start considering everything their Alpha had to fix, but they'd been making decent progress until the Cascade Range Pack had started causing problems.

Kai had already made his declaration to the Cascade Alpha. There was going to be a war even if the northern pack backed off. They'd done too much damage to walk away without some kind of retribution.

Sage and Jacob had nearly died, and then the Cascade Range Pack had started biting humans in their territory – causing chaos and dangerous situations. Now the Blue Mountain Pack had almost twenty wolves that were about to go through their first full moon in a few weeks.

It was a fucking nightmare.

Despite all that bullshit, Kai had taken over the situation with the strip club after the lion Alpha had dealt with the issue, thanks to *his* new mate, Kitty.

Mates seemed to be everywhere these days.

Noah checked his phone out of boredom and saw a text from Alexander asking if he was all right. The big wolf must have been talking to his witch mate again, because Lily was nothing if not a matchmaker, and his disinterest in his own mate was worrying her.

He'd feel bad if he thought there was a chance he could find her and make things work, but the likelihood of that was so tiny, Noah had given up on the concept of his own mate completely.

Not that he'd told anyone that...not even Liam.

After the chaos with Liam's mate, he'd asked Lily to tell him about his own mate in private at some other point in time as long as she wasn't in any immediate danger. That had been the right choice and had allowed him to ensure Liam was able to manage his new, bossy, bitchy mate who would kill for both of them if she saw anything she didn't like.

Noah liked her a lot more than he thought he would, but he also hadn't anticipated her complete and total devotion to his twin and everything Liam held dear, or how quickly it had happened.

All it had taken was for Zoe to see how much Liam cared about his pack, and she'd been a goner.

That was never going to happen with his own mate. It was literally impossible unless...

No, there was no time for that right now. They had a war on their hands and baby wolves on top of all their normal duties.

A girl came up and relentlessly knocked on his window like she was too excited or wired to rein it in. Noah slid his gaze sideways and found the lion Alpha's mate grinning at him with her other two mates behind her.

Was he ever going to have a moment's peace again?

Noah rolled his window down and the scent of lions washed over him. It wasn't unpleasant but it still raised his hackles a bit. "What can I do for you, Ms. Kitty?"

The girl grinned at her mates over her shoulder like she'd somehow won something. "See, I told you he was the nicest one."

That made him uncomfortable, but Noah didn't argue with her because that was definitely the persona he put on for everyone.

One of the lions gave her this sweet, indulgent smile that made his teeth ache and Noah refocused on the girl who smelled like she was still human, which was kind of surprising considering she was now the Alpha female of her pride.

"Do you not like strip clubs?" Kitty asked, tilting her head to the side in an attempt to look innocent. It was anything but when paired with her sharp tone and the scent of disappointment.

"I don't like the smell of despair," he confessed, tapping his fingers on the steering wheel again. It always took him back to the bad times. "It's a bit much to stomach right now."

Something in her face eased and Kitty reached inside the car, placing her hand on top of his. Noah froze and stared at her tiny hand, wondering if the lions were going to bite his arm off for touching her.

"Is there anything I can do to help while we're still here?" Kitty asked, forcing his eyes from her hand to her face.

"You're already doing too much," Noah muttered, pulling his hand out from under hers. "Don't worry, we'll take care of the girls once they decide what they want to do. They're still getting paid while we renovate this place and find new management. Kai is planning on paying for rehab for those who need it, and they'll all get therapy."

It hadn't been easy to arrange with everything else going on, but it seemed that Cascade had finally stopped biting humans for a short reprieve.

They could start again at any moment, and the stress of that unknown hung over them all. Noah had nearly bitten all his fingernails off worrying about it. Thankfully, his shifter healing repaired the damage before anyone could see it, but the tips of his fingers wouldn't stop aching from all the abuse.

"I'm not worried about the girls," Kitty told him, giving him this big, bright smile that was nearly blinding. "I know Kai will take care of them. Your pack just needs some help getting through the rough patches. Which reminds me, Calvin wants to know if he has time for a meeting? We need to discuss those bitten wolves."

There it was – the reason for his raised hackles. This was *their* territory, and no matter how much help the pride was, the lions were butting their nose into pack business and assuming they couldn't handle their own shit.

"Why don't you have your Alpha contact my Alpha?" Noah grabbed his phone to distract himself from his anger, not wanting to start a new problem out of his hurt pride. "I'm too low on the pecking order to bring requests like that to Kai. Didn't you know? I'm just the errand boy."

The two lions behind her growled, pissed off that Noah was being so disrespectful, but Kitty just tilted her head again. "I'm human and I really don't know that much about paranormal culture if I'm going to be honest with you. So, I'm sorry I wasn't aware, but it seems like you're a lot more important than that since you're here. Right?"

Noah wished she would just go away. She was far too optimistic for his current mood. "I'm here because my brother is here, and Liam is here because Zoe is. That's all."

Why was he being so fucking pessimistic? It wasn't like him to let that part of him out like this, and if he was right, this girl was going to make his misery her problem until he was just as bright and happy as her mates.

Noah would say it was impossible, but he'd seen the change in Calvin. He supposed that was the power of a mate.

"Well, I'm sure it's not that simple if the pride is any indication," Kitty told him, leaning on the car door. "Every single member in the pride is important. We couldn't do what we do without them."

She wasn't wrong, but Noah didn't want to think about it. Things were more complicated than whether she was right or not. Their pack was too small, and the stakes were too high for this bullshit.

"I appreciate your concern," Noah told her, texting his twin to hurry the fuck up. "I'm sure Kai will make time for your mate."

Kitty pushed off the car and stared at him, clearly wondering if she should say something else, but one of the lions wrapped his arm around her shoulders.

"Thanks, man. Take care," Adam said, giving him a two-finger salute. "I'm sure we'll be seeing each other soon."

Adam and Kitty disappeared into the strip club, but the other lion, the pride's Third and enforcer, lingered.

"It's my job to keep my pride members safe," Damien told him, crossing his arms over his chest, and glaring at Noah. "Considering how submissive you are, you'd know the full scope of your pack better than most."

Noah couldn't hide his flinch. Very few understood that, especially the ones at the top of the pack. So, why was this lion enforcer whose dominance was practically suffocating him bringing this up?

"Jacob and his mate Sage have visited the family side of the pride a few times now to see his parents. They've been talking about moving back to the Blue Mountain Pack." Damien looked away, eyes on the strip club. A look of disgust passed over his face. "I'm more of a realist than Kitty and Adam, so I want you to be straight with me."

His parents had been a huge deal for Jacob. He'd been so wrapped up in his mate and his pack that he hadn't gone to visit them when the pride first arrived in Portland, and Noah had a sneaking suspicion that wasn't the only reason.

Seeing them reminded him of the sister he couldn't save, and his parents couldn't stand the memory of the child they'd lost. That they were considering moving back...

Noah rubbed his temples and sighed. This was honestly the last thing they needed right now.

"Is it safe for them to move back?" Damien asked, watching him closely. "I don't want them to end up fodder for war."

Jacob's parents weren't that old, so they'd certainly be helpful when it came to the territory dispute with Cascade. Knowing them, they'd be insulted not to be included, but integrating them back into the pack would be just as annoying as dealing with all the newly bitten wolves who were still barely more human.

Even Amelia had her human moments and she'd taken to the wolf better than almost anyone except Sage.

Why hadn't Jacob mentioned this? Was he trying to hide it from Kai because he knew how stressful it would be? Was he trying to placate his parents, but ultimately hoping to convince them to stay with the pride?

"If you want me to be honest with you, then you should know that I think you, your pride, and your pretty little mate should leave Portland as soon as possible. Today if you can. This state isn't going to be safe for anyone until a victor is declared. And if Cascade wins...you should avoid the entire Pacific Northwest just like you did when those assholes ruled the Blue Mountain Pack."

It was way more than he should say to an outsider, but the Cirque de Nuit pride wasn't like other shifters. They were something unique and special that didn't look down on other races of shifters, the smaller shifters, or the mingling of different paranormal races.

They were a Sanctuary after all, and no one could

be denied sanctuary if requested unless doing so endangered everyone in said Sanctuary.

One life could not be worth more than many...or at least, that was the idea.

"I see." Damien uncrossed his arms and sighed. "Well, if they request a transfer, Calvin won't deny it. But I'll try to talk some sense into them. The newly bitten wolves would be welcome within our pride as well. That's what Calvin wants to talk to Kai about."

"Not your departure? We've delayed your schedule for long enough." Noah nearly crushed his phone when he saw his brother's middle finger emoji in response to his text. He was going to beat the shit out of Liam the next chance he got.

"Nah, Kitty was the reason for our delay, and now she wants to help you. We don't know how to say no to her." For the first time, Damien smiled, and Noah was fascinated by the way it changed his face.

He would never understand why mates were such a powerful thing in a shifter's life. Why had they been created this way and no one else? Why not *all* shifters? Fate was such a cruel bitch.

"Anyways, I'll let your brother know you're ready to get out of here," Damien said, reaching out with his fist.

Noah stared at it, not sure when the enforcer had decided they were close enough for this kind of ridiculous masculine display. Still...

He bumped his own fist against Damien's and resisted the absurd laughter he could feel bubbling up.

"Tell Lily we miss her, and we'll be seeing her soon."

"Will do."

Noah watched the lion walk up to the door of the strip club and take a deep breath, his face a bit green thanks to the scents of the place if he were right. No doubt the memories of what the previous owner had done to Kitty weren't easy to stomach either.

It must be nice to have a mate who could love you back, even if you had to go through hell for her.

Noah wished he were so lucky, but his mate wasn't capable of love, and that's why he'd decided he'd never go looking for her.

What raven would fall for a wolf anyway?

2

HARPER

Perched on the roof of the strip club, she watched the wolf in the car speak to the lions and their little human mate. He looked tense, and his aura told her a variety of things she doubted even his twin could pick up on.

This one was depressed and angry, but she couldn't say what about, not yet.

Another week of recon and she'd have every single wolf in the Blue Mountain Pack pegged. By then, it would be a piece of cake to complete the job.

Harper felt her partner's wings ruffle against hers as she readjusted while they watched the lions walk into the strip club. Valentina was just as good as her and just as deadly.

Finding another raven who'd abandoned their Collective had felt like a sign. Harper really hadn't thought there were many out there like her who didn't want the burdens of an entire flock's expectations on her shoulders.

The jobs they took were what she'd call...under the table.

Harper didn't have an Administration to field her calls and vet the clients, or decide which jobs were worth taking and who they'd be assigned to. She didn't have the Enclave to decline a job that could put ravens in danger or upset their secret world either.

No, it was just her, her blades, and the money.

Only one thing had stayed with her after leaving the Collective, and that was the need for a partner. Harper refused to be an idiot and risk her life just because she wanted to be independent and go her own way.

No, Valentina respected her and understood how important a pairing was. Even without the expectations of the Enclave, they'd both sworn the oath that all ravens swore to their partners.

It was the only thing she'd decided to keep. Everything else was simply a result of her training, and with this one job, she'd be able to pay off her debt to the Collective and be truly free of them once and for all.

Harper couldn't wait. It was almost tempting enough to try to take out the one sitting in his car with that pitiful look on his face. He was weak and ripe for death. It was there in his aura – thoughts of suicide and murder.

If her emotions were on, she might feel some empathy for him, but Harper felt nothing as she stared at him.

He was pretty though, she'd give him that. The wolf had broad shoulders and a tapered waist that made her wonder just how tall he was. Harper could admire a good-looking man even if she didn't feel anything for him.

The lack of emotions only made the sex better, in her opinion.

All she had to worry about was what would satisfy her, and how to go about getting it. Nothing else mattered, and men were all too happy to comply, in her experience.

Could she get a taste before she had to take this one out? Maybe she'd keep him as a pet instead of the other way around. His pack was one of the many who had tried to keep assassins for themselves after all.

That was the main reason why she refused to work alone, even if she was good enough to go solo. Some ravens thought that sharing the payday wasn't worth it – ravens like the ones she'd grown up with.

But Harper wasn't that stupid.

Even a trio of ravens could get caught if they weren't vigilant. Whenever witch or demon magic got involved, ravens were at a disadvantage just like any other shifter, unless they had a witch or two in the flock to make them charms and the like.

Then there'd been a few hunters good enough to match a raven's skill. Not every assassin was cut out for the job, but Harper? Well, she'd been born for this.

A door slammed open, and the human girl mated to the lions skipped out with a massive grin on her face. Harper had to look away because her aura was blinding. It was bright and bubbly and full of so much love it made her want to gag.

Then the two partially responsible for that aura came out, flanking the human like her very own personal bodyguards.

If her employer had asked for her to take down the Cirque, she would have refused. Even Harper wouldn't take on a job that endangered a Sanctuary. If the Sanctuaries were violated, it would destroy the careful rules of their coexistence.

After all, it was the only place she'd ever be accepted after leaving her Collective behind.

Then a man who looked nearly identical to the one in the car stepped out with a tiny little woman who hadn't yet had her first shift into her animal form. The red in her aura told Harper she had a prickly personality and was aggressive and most likely dominant.

It was edged with this rosy pink though that seemed to expand every time she looked at the one called Liam. The same love in the human girl's aura was in the wolf's, except it wasn't quite so blinding.

Harper was fascinated with the difference in the twin's auras though. They could not be more different.

Liam's was a bright, grassy green that was nearly as blinding as the human's. That green only got brighter when he saw his brother too, and even the prickly human's had this platonic affectionate tinge of orange when she saw Noah.

Noah's aura didn't change when he saw them except to get even darker until the blue was nearly a bruised purple – practically black even in the middle of this gorgeous March afternoon.

But his face didn't match his aura at all. He gave his twin a small smile and watched the girl, Zoe, climb in the back of the vehicle with a soft look on his face.

How much of his facial expressions were genuine?

The dark blue and purple were overwhelming, but it wasn't the only thing in his aura. The rest was just buried and roiling underneath like a nest of vipers pissed and ready to lash out the second they saw an opening.

Fascinating.

These three were staying in the city, and occasionally two others came to visit. They were the only ones who were easily accessible.

She and Valentina had already done recon on their private land, and the protection spells on it were something else. They even had demon magic wards, which was going to cause problems if they couldn't lure them off their land.

They wouldn't get paid unless every single wolf in the pack was taken down. That was the deal. If they accomplished that, they'd receive a fat paycheck that was enough to pay off her debt and retire.

Harper would never have to work another day in her life if she didn't want to.

There were a few other options, but Valentina wasn't too keen on them.

A slight ruffle warned her, and they took off in tandem as the car pulled out of the parking lot. She flew high enough above the vehicle that she wouldn't set off their instincts and followed as they made their way through the city.

They made a few more stops before ending the day at a townhome in Portland that was cute and had a lot of Victorian charm, if one cared about that sort of thing.

She aimed for the roof across from their home and shifted just before landing. Harper dropped into a crouch on the ledge and rested her arms on her knees as she watched the three of them walk up the stoop into the building.

The female and the male discussed dinner while the quiet twin said nothing, trailing behind them with that stupid smile on his face that did nothing to hide the emptiness in his eyes.

"You're moping," the female snapped, turning around before going through the door. "What's wrong with you, Noah?"

"Zoe," the other one warned. "Let's not get into a fight before dinner. You know how mean Noah is when he's hungry, and he didn't eat the sandwich."

"It's not my fault he's an idiot," Zoe snapped, crossing her arms over her chest. "Spit it out."

Harper grinned. She enjoyed this girl's sass. It cut right through the bullshit like one of her blades through flesh and bone.

"Nothing's wrong, Zoe," Noah assured. His voice was soothing as he tried to usher her into the house. "It's sweet you care though."

"Talk to Lily about your mate again so you can get this over with already," Zoe grumbled, smacking Noah's hand away. "You'll never know if it'll work unless you find her."

The mopey twin sighed and gave his brother a *look* that made Harper want to laugh even if she wasn't sure why. The one with the green aura winced and picked up his mate like they were newlyweds.

When he carried her over the threshold, Harper felt something like a pang in her chest and she tilted her head to the side as she considered the one with the blue aura.

It was extremely unusual for a wolf shifter to know they had a mate but do nothing about it. For most shifters, mates were the be-all and end-all of their existence, and nothing was more important than finding them.

So why was this one avoiding it?

Thankfully, ravens didn't have mates, not like all the other shifters. Sure, one could end up mated to a wolf or a trio of leopards or lions, but much like witches, ravens weren't born with a mate.

Noah...he looked so forlorn now that he was alone. His acting was pretty good, but Harper could see through the cracks in his façade. That was probably what the nurse had picked up on after a lifetime of dealing with patients.

His eyes darted upward, and she went completely still as he seemed to see straight into her soul. That was impossible though, thanks to the charm she'd purchased for a pretty penny. Harper was invisible to all the senses a shifter could possibly use.

But that didn't change the fact that it felt like he could see her.

Then he disappeared inside the townhome and Harper slowly let out a breath and took her hand off the knife she hadn't even realized she'd been reaching for.

What an intense presence for a submissive wolf.

"We can take them out now and lure the others

here with the mystery of their whereabouts," Valentina murmured, the words almost too quiet to hear. "The pack can hide on their land behind their fancy wards all they want, but there's nothing they can do against a sniper rifle."

Valentina used to be known for her skill with long-distance kills. Her record had been over thirteen miles once, but she'd attributed it to the charmed bullets and the direction of the wind. Still, it was incredibly impressive considering how much Harper preferred the up close and personal kill.

If she couldn't see the light leaving their eyes and their soul leaving their body, did it even really happen?

"We could split up," Harper murmured, replaying the little drama on those steps again and again. "The job would be done in a few days that way."

"Once more of them are dead, we'll split up," Valentina agreed. "Right now, they have too many friends. Between the Cirque and the witches, we'd be risking too much if we moved without reducing their numbers."

Another reason she'd paired up with Valentina. The other raven was far more level-headed and strategic. She didn't have issues controlling unpredictable impulses.

Like all ravens, Harper was drawn to the shiny and mysterious. But unlike most, she couldn't always deny the urge to take those things for herself, whether it was a good idea or not. Too many times she'd nearly made a perilous mistake because she'd been too distracted.

It looked like this Noah was going to be another diamond she couldn't resist, which was why she wanted to kill him as quickly as possible and eradicate the temptation.

"Should we move on them tonight?" Harper asked, checking the various blades on her person. "I'm getting bored with recon. These wolves are so fucking predictable."

"We could." Valentina jumped up on the ledge beside Harper and stood tall, her shadow spreading until it touched the building across the street. "Depends on what you want to do though. It would be on you to go in there and slit their throats while they sleep. I'll be here for backup, of course, but that route includes more waiting."

"And the other?" Harper really hoped they'd go with the first one, but their partnership only worked because they both listened to each other and made the best decision for their pair, not the individual.

"We go undercover in their little town. It would give us access to more of the pack. We could take them out first, and then circle back to Portland. These three are sitting ducks, Harper. It's child's play."

Valentina was right. This would be too easy, but...

That fucking wolf was a shiny little toy and Harper

wanted to snatch it for herself just to see if it would be as easy to make him cry as she thought it might be.

"Let's do another day of recon," she suggested. "Tomorrow we'll make our decision after reevaluating their town and private land."

Leaving that forlorn little wolf alive was a bad idea. Harper knew her own weaknesses better than most but taking precautions would ensure they didn't make the same mistakes the last ravens who got entangled with this pack had.

Taking them all out in one fell swoop was the only way, or she could kiss her freedom goodbye.

Harper would rather die than end up as someone's pet. Never again would her life belong to someone else.

3

NOAH

Their night was relatively boring. Noah had helped Liam cook while Zoe organized all the files of the new wolves as well as the girls from the club. She hadn't been at this for very long, but the woman already had it all down pat.

It was impressive and Noah couldn't help feeling grateful all over again that his brother had ended up with such a competent mate. It was nothing less than he deserved after all the bullshit they'd gone through over the years.

Liam had desperately needed Zoe to put herself between him and the rest of the pack though he'd never admit it. His twin had always done everything he could for Kai, Olivia, and Alexander, even if it was slowly killing him.

The only reason Noah had gone along with it all

was because they owed Shane a life debt, and he'd always had a soft spot for the gentle giant who'd tried to kill them one night thanks to their idiocy.

Alexander's mate was perfect for him too.

Noah really didn't think anyone else could have accepted a witch so easily. It didn't bother the wolf at all, which was surprising considering how long one had kept him trapped in his wolf form.

He supposed killing one's abuser was certainly more therapeutic than most wanted to admit out loud.

They were supposed to be the good guys after all. Condoning murder was frowned upon.

But if Kai left that human alive who'd abused all those girls at the strip club, Noah would go hunt him down on his own terms. There was no room for people like that in his territory.

Not anymore.

It didn't matter that he was one of the most submissive wolves in the pack. Noah was a vicious asshole when he was backed into a corner, and he was starting to feel that hunger for blood all over again.

This time, he wouldn't have his brother to watch out for him either. Liam was lost in his brand-new mate bond and completely blissed out. As he should be at a time like this.

Which was one of the main reasons why Noah was so fucking pissed this war with Cascade had dragged out long enough to affect his brother's honeymoon phase with his mate.

They should have taken care of the problem after they'd tried to kill Jacob. That had been the time to act.

Now Kai was trying to find a way around an all-out war, so they didn't get the Council on their asses. He shook his head and wished things were easier.

It didn't help that he'd woken up with fuzzy memories of strange dreams that seemed to fade even more when he tried to reach for them. All he could remember was a pair of luminescent brown eyes that had never once blinked.

Even the memory made his skin crawl, and Noah picked up his phone again. No news from the homestead made him anxious.

Liam and Zoe were in their room, locked up in there with state-of-the-art soundproofing, thank goodness. The last thing he needed was to hear them fucking.

Once again, something had his hackles rising for no reason and Noah whipped around, studying the big bay window in the living room for the thousandth time. Just like yesterday, it felt like someone was watching him.

He walked over to the glass and pulled back the curtain, studying the street as well as the rooftops of the buildings.

Witches might be walking around, or it could be

any number of shifters currently under their protection.

Frank, their resident bear shifter, had already agreed to help protect their territory. He'd packed up and left the day before which meant there shouldn't be any predators left in the city that should have Noah feeling like this.

Maybe he was just being paranoid.

Then his phone rang, making him jump like a fucking idiot.

"What can I do for you, Lily?" he asked, inspecting the street and the rooftop of the condo building across the way one last time.

"How are you doing in the city?" she asked, sounding hesitant. "How's my sister?"

"A peach, as always." Noah closed the curtains but still couldn't shake the feeling he was being watched. "How are things over at the homestead?"

"Kai is going to be announcing his decision soon." Lily sounded anxious and was chewing on her nails again if he was right. "Alexander doesn't know I called you."

"I'm not interested in getting between mates," he warned her, ready to hang up before he could hear whatever secrets she wanted to whisper into his ear. "I love you, Lily, and I'd do anything for you, but I won't lie to Alexander, or hide anything from him."

"I'm not asking you to," she snapped, that attitude

back in an instant. "I'm calling you about *your* mate, stupid."

He narrowed his eyes and went through the entire townhouse again to make sure there were no weak points. The magic seemed to be holding up too, thanks to that witch, Morgan.

Maybe he should call her and double-check because this feeling had saved his ass more times than he could count.

"I know you don't want to talk about it, but I think we should," Lily said, sounding as bossy as ever.

"Why wouldn't you tell Alexander about this? Seems weird." Noah hummed under his breath as he went up the stairs and passed his brother's room before going up to the third floor.

"I haven't told anyone about the specifics of your mate." Lily huffed, just like she had when he'd asked her to keep it to herself. "But I think you should, considering what is about to go down."

He froze on the landing of the third floor as he processed what she was getting at. "No."

"Why not?" Now she was whining.

Noah rolled his eyes and checked the empty bedrooms before taking the stairs up to the roof. "I don't like what you're implying."

"And what am I implying, Noah?" Lily was all worked up now and she sounded like a pissed-off cat after a bath.

He pushed the door open and took a deep breath, closing his eyes to sift through the infinite scents the city offered up to his sensitive nose. Best one in the pack, if he did say so himself.

Liam may be the more empathetic one who carried the emotional baggage of their pack, but Noah had been the one who could track anything and everything. He'd been the front line of their defense for so long thanks to this secret they'd kept from everyone.

Even Kai.

Only Liam, Alexander, and Shane knew how good his nose was, and Noah had planned to let his new Alpha know all the things that made him different from his twin, but they'd waited to make sure this wouldn't end up like all the other Alphas. Then the timing had never quite been right once they were sure.

Opening his eyes allowed the setting sun to sear his retinas, but Noah didn't bother looking away as he stared at the condo building across the street again.

Why was he so sure that's where this bad feeling was coming from? There was nothing on the air that told him shit, but Noah knew witches could mask their scents if they wanted.

"You're implying we can use my mate to help us win this war, and I refuse to find her just to get down on my knees and beg for her to save us. We both know that wouldn't work anyway, and we don't have the money to hire a raven."

If he could even find a way to contact her.

Ravens were notoriously secretive. Almost no one knew where their eyries were tucked away. Just like the fox dens, they existed in strange pockets of the universe.

How was he going to get a line to her? By calling the Enclave? Noah highly doubted the ruling council for ravens would entertain a mate bond that could take one of their precious assassins away from them.

And why an assassin? Noah couldn't think of a single thing they would have in common. Maybe the universe was playing a cruel joke and wanted to give him the death he'd toyed with for the last decade.

They did say that the only time you ever saw a raven's red eyes was because they were there to kill you.

"Fine, maybe that was a bad idea," Lily conceded. "But I still think you should try to find her. I could ask Calvin to look into it. We've helped more ravens than you'd think in the Cirque. I'm pretty sure there are two flocks in the Pacific Northwest alone."

"Well, you'd certainly know better than me." Noah decided the plants on the roof needed to be watered, and the solar panels should be cleaned off, so he went to work, holding the phone between his shoulder and ear. "But I'm not interested in finding her, Lily. So, if that's all you want to talk about, I'm going to go. I've got shit to do."

"You know, you can be such a dick," she muttered. "I honestly hadn't expected that."

"And yet, you still want me to paint the mural in your living room." Noah shook his head but couldn't help his smile. He liked the witch a lot more than he thought he would when she'd first come to the homestead.

"Why won't you let me pay for that?" she snapped, clearly embarrassed. "It's so much work."

"Consider it my mating gift to you and Alexander." He took the hose out first and started watering the plants, noting which ones needed to be harvested. "Can you do something for me, Lily?"

"Anything, Noah. Just name it."

She was going to regret saying that.

"Can you destroy the information I know you've saved regarding my mate? Just torch it, and then put it in one of those protection boxes. I don't want anyone going to look for her on my behalf."

The silence stretched for what felt like forever, but Noah had no intention of breaking it. None of this seemed to bother him the same way it bothered everyone else – including Zoe.

For someone who'd been so against the idea of fated mates, she'd sure as hell accepted it as the one thing in the paranormal world that made sense to her. There were still times he caught her muttering about the physics of the human to wolf shift, as well as the complications that could occur but never did...

But a mate? For whatever reason, that made a lot more sense to her.

A raven assassin was someone he knew couldn't love him, and even if she could, Noah didn't think he could ever get past what he'd been forced to endure thanks to ravens.

It was a no-win situation, and he wasn't interested in dealing with that kind of drama, especially not during a war.

"Are you sure?" Lily finally asked.

He'd moved on to the little plant mister and sprayed the more delicate ones, knowing the green witch on the phone could sense if he lied thanks to the various plants she'd put on the roof and throughout the house.

"Just lock it up. I don't want to be tempted. Liam and Zoe need me here. Our new little wolf has decided that I'm part of her mate bond with Liam. It's kind of sweet actually, considering how mean she is to everyone else."

Lily actually snorted at that. "She reminds me a lot of my sister, and Laura fucking loves her, so I'm not surprised she'd adopt you two. Zoe has a big heart, she's just rough around the edges."

"Go make sure Alexander isn't going to do something stupid and call me the second you hear news. I don't like having to wait for this shit to trickle down just because we're in the city."

"I heard Kai might be sending out two of the newly bitten to help you guys," Lily whispered, her hand covering her mouth if he were right.

"You live with wolves. They can all hear you," he reminded her, setting the mister down.

Noah got started on harvesting, setting the fruits and veggies to one side, and all the witchy and medicinal herbs to the other.

"How do you feel about sharing some of these herbs with Zoe? She's surprisingly good at herbal medicine too."

"You can split everything into three piles," Lily instructed. "I'll have the new wolves bring some of the rarer pieces for the witches in Portland and Laura. Try not to be too mean to them."

"As long as they have half a brain, I won't have to be."

"So rude for the wolf who welcomed us all with open arms," Lily teased. "Make sure you get some sleep, Noah, or I'll tell Zoe to drug you."

He glared at the little pot of turtles on a string that was a propagation of the one in her living room. "Do it and I'll tell Alexander you're ready for pups."

Lily gasped in horror. "You wouldn't."

Noah couldn't help his grin. They both know he would.

"Fine! You prick. Just don't kill yourself and we have a deal."

His hands paused as he considered her choice of words. Had she tried to scry for him again without saying anything?

"I'll do my best," he promised, glad that Alexander had such a perfect mate. "Tell Damien I appreciated his honesty when you see him. I need to finish with these plants. So go eat something and make sure Olivia does too. Without Liam and me there, it's bound to be a mess."

"You're not wrong," she muttered, hanging up the phone without a goodbye.

He liked that about her.

Noah was extremely pleased with all the mates they'd gotten over the last few months, but Olivia hadn't found hers yet despite being the Third. It was weird, but she was the only one who hadn't asked for their new resident witch to take a look.

At first, he'd thought it was a mistake not to, but now that he knew who his own mate was, he couldn't agree more. She'd find her mate when the time was right, or she wouldn't.

Until then, she didn't have to worry about keeping someone else alive who was more precious than her own soul.

If something happened to Zoe, Liam wouldn't survive it, not even with Noah at his side to try to keep him together. That's just the way things were, and it was kind of a terrifying thought now that he had to contemplate a future without his own mate.

Well, he supposed it could be worse. She could always outright reject him and mean it.

Noah sat on the lounge chair and started sorting the herbs as he stared at his phone and the contact currently displayed.

Should he call her?

This was probably something he should ask the higher-ups about before contacting someone like Morgan, but Noah was pretty sure he was the only one currently losing his goddamn mind.

He paused when he realized Lily had told him to make three piles. Had she known what he had planned? Sure, the third one could be for her, but Lily had all these plants at her greenhouse already.

Crazy-ass witches.

Noah shook his head and tapped Morgan's contact.

Six months ago, he would have never thought he could like them so much, but here he was, friends with witches and close enough with them he could call one that had the kind of power to keep demons off his property.

"I was expecting you to call," Morgan purred the moment she picked up the phone. "What took you so long?"

4

HARPER

Why was this one wolf so intuitive despite all her magic?

Valentina was checking out La Grande on her own and Harper was supposed to keep an eye on the wolves in the city, but they'd done nothing interesting after calling a bear shifter.

That bear could be problematic, but not if they ensured they wouldn't cross paths with him. He wasn't on the kill list after all.

If they had to, Valentina would take him out with one of her special bullets enchanted with the kind of magic that would take down anything short of a demon.

Launching off the roof she'd been watching them from all day, Harper circled high above, eyeing the wolf harvesting herbs of all things.

His aura was different today. There was less of that bruised purple and the navy blue better suited his melancholy demeanor in her opinion.

Harper wondered if he could sense her somehow, because he looked up, right at her, like he knew *exactly* where she was.

"Morgan, that's never going to feel normal," she heard him say, eyes dropping back down to the herbs. "I wasn't sure you'd want to hear from someone like me."

"I have a vested interest in your survival," the woman on the other end of the line said with this seductive voice that made Harper's skin crawl. "You can call me whenever you want."

Who the fuck was this girl, and what kind of relationship did she have with this wolf?

Harper landed on the far side of Noah's roof in her raven form. Even this close, there was no way he should scent, hear, or see her, thanks to the charms around her neck.

She'd bought as much magic as she could afford and then some. Harper didn't want anyone finding her, especially her old Collective.

Even still, the wolf glanced over his shoulder in her general direction, but his eyes didn't lock onto her. It made her extremely uncomfortable.

What the fuck was he picking up on?

"I have a bad feeling we're being watched," Noah

confessed. "I'm not a witch, so it's not like I can check the wards on the townhouse. There's nothing I can scent or see either. Am I fucking crazy?"

The woman was quiet as Noah finished sorting through the herbs. When he started tying them up in bundles to dry, she finally chose to spoke.

"Why aren't you on the homestead, Noah?" the woman's voice was a lot sharper and meaner than Harper had expected considering the softness she'd heard earlier.

"Calvin turned over the strip club to us, and we can't just abandon our territorial duties, *Morgan*," Noah snapped. "There are a lot of people who rely on us to protect them. I'm surprised you didn't See it."

The name Morgan tickled her memory and Harper decided she needed to know more about this witch, especially if she could See clearly enough to know this wolf planned to call her.

"I should have known better than to trust a bunch of wolves to follow instructions," the woman muttered. "You're worse than cats, I fucking swear."

"I'm offended." But this time, Noah didn't actually sound offended and for some reason that tickled her.

Harper actually giggled.

"Why can I get leopards to follow instructions then?" she demanded. "And yet I can't even get wolves to update me when they choose to do something fucking stupid?"

"Because wolves aren't used to working in groups quite the same way your felines do. Should I expect a visit then?"

It was hilarious how nonchalant Noah was about something he should definitely be more concerned about.

He'd been the same way the night before when he'd woken up – just sat up straight, right out of a dead sleep and stared at her crouched on his windowsill like it was totally normal.

Harper still couldn't believe he'd asked her to come inside. She'd told him to go back to sleep and that she'd watch over him, and he'd believed her. Then she'd taken the memory of that moment from him, but it seemed like maybe...

This one might actually remember some of it if he was still so sensitive around her, even though he couldn't see or smell her. For a wolf – not being able to use their nose was worse than death.

It didn't seem to affect him though. Not when he could sense her somehow despite having all the magic in the world to erase her existence. Harper wondered if he could sense her even in the shadow realm.

That would be a fun game to play and might keep her from falling asleep while she had to watch over them.

"Yeah, I'll be there as quickly as I can, but I live pretty far away. Maybe I should call in a favor."

"I can ask one of the pride members to give you a ride," Noah suggested, taking the herbs he'd tied together to one of the cupboards where they could dry. "I know you don't like to drive."

Definitely a witch based on all the little details, but there was nothing that quite gave the clan ones away like their innate dislike for driving – almost like they missed the old days even if they couldn't remember them.

Witches used to fly with ravens, but that had been a very long time ago, per the librarian in her old Collective.

A lot of things had changed over the last few hundred years, and yet, Harper preferred the freedom of a world without an Administration or Enclave telling her how to breathe and sleep and live.

"Nah, I don't need a ride. I'll figure it out." The witch hung up before the wolf could say anything more, and Harper shifted from her raven form to her human one.

Was she going to have to take out a clan witch too? This was starting to get way more complicated than their original agreement. Harper really didn't want to get on the bad side of witches when her survival was so dependent on witches being willing to sell their magic to her.

"I have to be losing my mind," the wolf muttered, tossing his phone onto the lounge chair.

Harper couldn't resist the way his blue eyes darkened until they matched his aura whenever he was alone. She couldn't stop wondering how soft that fluffy black hair would be either and she kept catching herself admiring how broad his shoulders were.

Was he strong enough to pin her down? Was he fast enough to catch her before she slit his throat?

This wolf was so delicious she wanted to take a bite out of him. Killing him before she had a taste would be a total waste and Harper had always been taught that one shouldn't be inefficient.

"I don't think you're losing your mind," she murmured, eyes narrowing as she waited to see if he could hear her despite the charm.

Strangely, he didn't react to the direction of the noise that was stolen by the charm around her neck, but his shoulders tensed.

"I actually think you're the only one here with any brains," she whispered, sliding off the ledge of the roof.

The moment her boots hit the ground, his eyes were on her, just like the night before – but this time the pretty blue was glowing the same silver as the moon when it was at its fullest.

"What the *fuck* is that?" he muttered, narrowing his eyes as if he could somehow force her into focus.

"A phantom." She grinned when his gaze followed her across the rooftop. "Or perhaps a death omen."

This wasn't going to end well, but Harper couldn't

resist. Especially when he was so pretty. She slid into the shadow realm and slipped off the necklace, wrapping her fingers around the charms as she carefully picked her way through the plants that were scattered everywhere.

Noah's shoulders were practically at his ears now, but he couldn't figure out where she was – not in the shadow realm. That was something at least.

She walked across the roof and stopped when they were close enough she could slip her blade between his ribs and right into his heart before he ever realized she was there.

The moment she left the shadow realm, he inhaled sharply, eyes dropping to her face even if they couldn't focus.

So, the charms were useless with him to some degree. Why was that?

Then she did something reckless and stupid and definitely not boring.

Harper dropped her charms and watched for the exact moment his eyes finally focused on hers.

The wolf didn't jump back or scream when he saw her glowing red eyes. He just stopped breathing.

It was fucking adorable.

"Why can you tell where I am when I'm wearing magic?" she asked, planting her hands on her hips. She even leaned forward, and he leaned back so the distance between them remained the same.

But he didn't retreat.

"A raven?" he asked, almost like he couldn't believe it. There was a hint of something else too, but Harper couldn't quite put her finger on what it was.

The only thing that gave her some insight was his aura, but the thing was roiling like she'd kicked a hornet's nest.

"A murder," she corrected, grinning up at him. "A wolf?"

His eyes widened, almost like he couldn't believe she'd ask such a stupid question. "Are you here to kill me?"

"I am." Harper straightened and let her eyes wander from his head to his toes, and then all the way back up.

His pecs were right in her fucking face, and they were massive. She was reaching out before she could think twice, and Harper squeezed both of them, admiring their heft.

Noah made this strange little noise in the back of his throat, but he didn't try to stop her either.

"I think your tits are bigger than mine," she observed, giving them one last squeeze. "I have to admit, that's impressive."

"Okay, that's enough of that." Noah slapped her hands away and gave her this amusing look of disbelief. "Why didn't you just kill me then? Why do...this?"

She looked up into his eyes, but they didn't tell her

as much as his aura did. "I wanted to know why you could sense me even when I wear enough magic to erase myself from existence. My presence woke you up last night. That's extremely unusual. Are you some special breed of wolf? I've heard there are some wolf witches around somewhere."

His mouth was still hanging open and she grinned, tapping his chin to close it for him.

Precious.

She was definitely going to take a bite out of this one.

"Show me your eyes," he demanded, gripping her shoulders hard enough to hurt.

"But, sweetheart, I already am." Harper batted her eyelashes up at him and laughed when he shook her. Stupid, but definitely not boring. "Okay, okay fine."

When she blinked, the glowing red disappeared, and then she looked like nothing more than a human in the light of dusk.

Noah didn't release her, which was even more interesting. He wasn't afraid of her either even though she'd already told him she was there to kill him. No, this idiot was more interested in the color of her eyes.

"So, did I dream of you?" he murmured, head tilting like a puppy's. "I definitely remember these eyes."

That wasn't good.

Harper brushed his hand off her and went over to

the pile of fruits and vegetables he'd harvested. She selected one of the plumpest blueberries and popped it into her mouth as she considered why this wolf was different than all the others.

Only certain witches could detect a raven, and even then, they had to be stronger than whoever had created whatever charms the raven might be wearing. And Harper had gone to one of the most powerful witches she could find.

There were only a handful that should be able to sense her.

"It wasn't a dream," she told him, selecting another blueberry. "I simply took the memory, but it seems you've retained a fraction of it." Grinning at him over her shoulder, she popped the tart fruit into her mouth. "So greedy."

He blinked and then frowned. "Why haven't you killed me yet?"

She shrugged and selected a few more before sauntering over to him. "It's not time." Then she offered him a blueberry.

Noah didn't look away from her face though. "I like your orange hair. It suits you and really makes the honey in your eyes pop."

She tossed the blueberry into her mouth and wondered why he'd focus on that. "My mother hated it."

This time, it was Noah who took a step forward. "Why's that?"

"It doesn't make me very forgettable, now does it?" She offered him another blueberry, and he actually reached for it.

Harper pulled it back, forcing him closer. "Say 'ah.'"

The silver in his eyes mellowed until it was back to his human blue. She watched it slip from the deep navy to something almost icy.

Noah opened his mouth and leaned in, giving her every opportunity to place the fruit directly on his tongue. "Ah."

So, she did.

His tongue wrapped around her fingers and Harper shivered at the silky-smooth sensation. Why wasn't he trying to run from her?

Then he wrapped his fingers around her wrist and studied her just as intently as she was studying him. "Who did I piss off to earn a raven contract?"

"No one in particular." Harper could easily pull out of his gentle grip, but his fingers were warm against the chilly March air. "Not that I should be telling you anything at all."

"Why are you then?" His whole body seemed to strain forward until he was looming over her, closing the distance between them until his scent was in her nose and Harper couldn't resist breathing in the smell of sharp pine.

"You're pretty," she admitted, resting her hand on his chest again just to feel the hard muscles underneath.

Wolves were so much bigger than ravens. It was crazy to see it up close and personal. Harper didn't think any of the male ravens she knew were quite this tall or broad, even as adults.

"You're prettier," Noah murmured, tugging on one of her curls so the hair bounced.

She looked up, surprised to hear truth in his voice. Even his aura was lighter until it matched the night sky. Harper could almost see stars in it if she looked hard enough.

"I promise you're sweeter," she teased, reaching up to touch his face.

His jaw was prickly, which was a shock considering how soft his skin looked.

"Hm, I doubt we have the same definition of sweet." Before she could respond to that, his other hand was wrapped around the nape of her neck and practically pulled her off her feet. "Can I have a taste?"

"Even though I'm supposed to kill you?" she asked, unable to look away from those full lips that were suddenly a lot closer.

"I'd rather know what you taste like before I die.

Then you can carve my heart from my chest and keep it for yourself. How does that sound?"

Harper couldn't believe there was a wolf in the world quite like this one. It was almost like...almost like he was made for her.

That thought had her snapping back to reality.

She jerked backward, but she'd already gotten too close, and this asshole was too strong. His grip on her neck tightened and he pressed his lips to hers hard enough she tasted blood.

Instantly, she melted at the sweet taste of him. There was the tang of blueberries, and something that was all his own – like spring water still icy cold and barely thawed.

His tongue slid into her mouth so expertly she barely even noticed the intrusion until it was stroking her own. Harper couldn't feel emotions, but she could certainly feel this.

It was like a bolt of lightning from her mouth straight to her pussy, and her body wanted more of it.

"Tell me, pretty little raven, would you let me taste you before you kill me?" Noah asked, his chest heaving as he tried to catch his breath. "It's all I can think about."

"Who am I to deny a man his dying wish?" she murmured, wrapping her arms around his neck.

And just like that, his aura went from the night sky to the creamy blue of dawn with breathtaking purple framing the edges. Noah even smiled down at her like she'd exceeded his expectations.

Then he dropped to his knees and pressed his face into her stomach.

Harper didn't know what to do with this. Never had she encountered anyone as crazy as this asshole. It was enough to rival her own insanity, but...

She slid her fingers through his fluffy black hair and sighed happily when it was just as soft as she'd imagined. Then she tightened her grip and yanked back so he was forced to look up at her.

"Now, be a good little puppy and make me scream."

5

NOAH

He was definitely losing his mind. That was the only explanation for the madness he felt when her scent filled his senses to the point that nothing else existed.

Feathers and blood and something almost sweet, like mangoes. It made him think of that bright orange hair cut into a curly bob that suited her perfectly.

What were the odds that he'd run into a raven? Were they even smaller than the chances that the one who happened to be stalking him was also his mate? That she was here at all had to mean something.

Well, there was only one way to find out.

Her grip on his hair was sharp and felt so good. He couldn't hold in the groan when she yanked him forward hard enough to sting, placing his nose right between her legs.

Oh, fuck, she had no idea what she was doing, but this little raven would soon find out that just because he was submissive, that didn't mean he couldn't be cruel and malicious while still doing exactly what she'd told him to do.

This was definitely a mistake, but he couldn't think past the fact that she was a raven – that she could be his mate, and that she was just so fucking gorgeous. She'd flirted with him all while promising him death.

Noah was a fucking goner.

He wrapped his arms around her legs and lifted her up, burying his face right where she wanted him. The scent of her was sweet and mouthwatering.

Every bit of fucking sense he might have had disappeared like mist on a hot summer morning.

Gently, he placed her on the empty lounge chair, fingers hooking in her waistband. When he pulled back, her pants came with him until they snagged on her boots.

Noah was too mesmerized to really care what she was feeling or thinking. If he was right, she felt nothing at all other than the physical pleasure he could give her, so he was going to enjoy every fucking second of this before he had to kill her, or she killed him.

Placing one foot on his shoulder, he turned to the other and unlaced her boot, sliding blades out of sheaths until there was nothing but her bare skin. He pressed his lips to that soft, silky skin that was such a pretty shade of honey-brown, just like her eyes.

Exquisite.

Then he removed her other boot and Noah scraped his teeth along the inside of her ankle, letting his eyes wander up the length of her legs to the sweet center. His canines elongated and he could feel his eyes shift from blue to silver again.

Soon his humanity would slide off his bones until there was only the wolf left behind. His teeth and claws ached, and Noah was so hungry...starving for the warmth she could give him.

Even if it was just this once – he'd make sure she would never forget him.

The way she grinned up at him in response was too much, and Noah couldn't be bothered to do slow anymore.

He attacked, mouth covering that soft, sweet bud, tongue diving into her center all as he sucked as much of her into his mouth as he could. His hands pressed her hips down into the chair and he ate her like she was the dessert he'd been promised on death row.

It was extremely satisfying to feel her hips lift, pressing herself into his mouth as soft little sighs escaped her. No doubt it was the only part of her that was soft.

Sliding a finger inside her, he licked his lips, eyes

closing as the sweetness became the only thing he could taste, smell, see, and feel.

He needed more before he lost his mind and took a bite out of her.

"Fuck, that's so good, puppy," she murmured, fingers stroking his hair as he licked and sucked and nibbled.

Noah didn't care that they were on a rooftop out in the open, or that his brother and his mate were downstairs in their own little slice of heaven. Not a single thought of the witch who was supposedly on her way either, or the duties he had to his pack.

Only her and this taste.

His dick was so hard it hurt, and nothing was going to make that better until he could fuck her so deep that he'd claim every inch of her inside and out.

Noah slid a hand up her stomach and gripped the top of her shirt, ready to rip the whole thing off so he could see those luscious tits under the rising moon.

"If you tear a single hole into any of my clothes, I'll slit your throat right here and now," she warned, pressing a sharp blade just below his jaw.

Noah was so far gone all he could do was growl as he rubbed his nose against her clit, barely seeing anything past the fabric and the need to get it off of her.

"So feral," she murmured, tipping his chin up with the knife.

He snarled, the claws at the tip of his fingers erupting as he forced her to stay right where she was.

Before he could figure out what the fuck was going on, Noah was on his back and she was on top of him, grinning as she adjusted until she was sitting on his face.

"Do a good job, and I'll let you fuck any hole, any way you want." The raven removed the blade from his neck and set it down so she could yank her shirt over her head. "You have five minutes, wolfie."

A challenge?

His tongue darted out to probe her center, feeling just how wet and ready she was.

Five minutes was more than enough.

Grabbing her ass, he yanked her forward until she was completely covering his face, and he sucked her clit into his mouth as he ground her against him.

Ride me, he was telling her. *Fuck my face until I suffocate, or you come.*

It was like she could read the thoughts going through his head, because her lips parted and she started gyrating above him, thighs trembling as he brought her closer and closer.

Until she collapsed on top of him into a squirming mess.

Jesus fucking Christ, she tasted so good that Noah didn't stop even then. His claws dug into her thighs and held her in place as he fucked her through her orgasm with his tongue.

"Oh, fuck, I had a feeling you'd be good at this," she groaned, fingers gripping his hair tight.

Again. He wanted her to come again.

Noah slid two fingers inside her and stroked that little spot inside that would have her losing her mind, sucking hard enough she might just gut him for it, but instead she started screaming.

This was even better.

Before she finished, he flipped her over and pressed her face down into the lounge chair to muffle those screams. Noah fingered her as he pulled himself out of his pants, licking the taste of her from his lips.

She was everywhere and it was more than he could take.

Noah slammed inside of her, gripping the back of her neck and shoving down until he had her pinned beneath him. "I'd say I did a good job, don't you?"

The sweet little raven nodded, pushing back against him. "Fuck me already."

But Noah had no plans to rush this, not when he'd likely never see her again. If she let him live, he'd probably lose all memory of this, and if she tried to kill him, he'd have to fight back.

Until then, they had this, and he planned to take everything he could from it.

"So sweet, I could eat you all day and night," he

whispered in her ear. He dragged his canines down her neck and over her shoulder, breathing her in until she'd replaced his soul with her own.

"At least you're good at it," she teased, pushing back against him again. "This part is making me wonder if that's all you got."

"I want to savor this," he admitted, running a hand down her bare back where tattoos decorated her spine. "I've never seen or tasted anything quite this exquisite. Almost makes me regret the death you promised me."

Surprisingly, she had nothing to say to that.

His hand pressed down on her lower back, forcing an arch. He gripped her hip tight with his other hand and yanked her back hard so she slammed onto his dick. The sound that came out of her told him he'd managed to hit that sweet spot just right.

"How many times do you think I can get you off?" he murmured, grinding his hips against her ass. "I'm hoping at least twice more. Then maybe I'll finally come."

"Just shut up and fuck me already," she snapped, reaching back for him.

"Ah-ah, you said any way I want, didn't you? You never specified how long or how many orgasms I was allowed to take."

Those honey-brown eyes glanced back at him with something like alarm, but he doubted she felt anything close to that considering how sweet and turned on she smelled.

There was no sharp hint of fear or apprehension either.

Not a single emotion on the air to tell him what she was thinking other than how good he could make her feel.

That was enough for him, at least for now.

Her scent was thick on his tongue as he slowly stroked in and out, hitting the spot that made her eyes roll back into her head every single time.

Fuck, she was so tight, and he was ready to burst, but watching her fall apart underneath him by doing exactly what she'd told him to do...

Noah was never going to forget this, even if she tried to take his memories again. There was just no way, not when his sensitive nose tasted that deep, musky flavor underneath it all that told him what he refused to accept or believe.

This was about the physical, nothing else.

His fingers found her clit and started rubbing little circles in time with each thrust and her body was just so responsive and sensitive that she was digging her nails into the cushion of the lounge chair in seconds.

The way her entire body clenched around his dick was almost too much and Noah gritted his teeth while he tried to get ahold of his own desires and urges.

He'd promised to fuck her long and hard until she

was just as lost as he was. He would make her lose her mind until she was forced to accept that no one else could get her off quite this good.

Maybe then she'd reconsider killing him if only so he could do it again.

She liked it rough too, because she came again when he slammed into her, and reached back for him.

He wrapped a hand around her neck and pulled her back against his chest, grinding against her sweet ass. His nose was buried in her neck, and he couldn't resist reaching around to squeeze one of her tits just like she'd done to him.

Fuck, he was going to lose it. The edge was right there, and he didn't think he could resist anymore, not when he she was fucking up his head with that smell.

Before he could stop himself, he was stroking into her hard and fast, about to explode any second. The bouncing of her tits and the little cries that left that swollen mouth sent him right over, and he came so hard his vision blacked out and Noah sank his teeth into her shoulder.

The ache finally eased, and the taste of her blood was almost as good as the sweetness still lingering on his tongue and chin.

"What the fuck is wrong with you?" she demanded, struggling to get free.

His wolf was having none of it, and Noah growled as he held her against him, dick still pulsing inside her.

The little raven was quivering like she was right on the edge of another orgasm and all he could think of was what it would take to push her over the edge *again* and *again* until she agreed to stay here with him forever.

This time she backed her words up with a knife.

Noah felt it slice through his skin, but it didn't hit anything vital – almost as if she were simply trying to warn him.

"Pretty, pretty mate," he rumbled, licking the blood from her shoulder. "My pretty little raven. Are you going to take my heart and hide it beneath your floorboards, hm? Are you finally going to put me out of my misery?"

She went completely still, and Noah started rubbing little circles into her clit again, so far gone in the scent and taste of her it was all he could think about.

"I can make you come again, and then you can kill me. How about that?" he whispered, kissing the brutal mark he'd left on her shoulder. "Just let me hold you a little bit longer."

He really hadn't expected her to let him, but he was still caught off guard when he was suddenly on his back again, but this time he landed on the ground with a *thud* and the hard jolt was just enough to release the hold she had on him.

Until she leaned down and fucked it all up by putting her neck too close to his nose.

"I'm no one's mate," she told him, hand on his throat to keep him pinned. "Not even yours."

His arms were longer than hers and it took almost nothing to pull her back down on his dick. "Sure, whatever you say, Ms. Raven."

"It's Harper," she snapped, breath hitching when he pressed up into her. "I'm going to kill you now, wolfie."

"One more time? Please, let me taste you one more time. I promise I'll be good. No biting or anything." Forcing her hips down and grinding her against him did exactly what he hoped it would.

That careful precipice she'd been teetering on was too narrow and she faltered when he pushed her right over the edge again.

"Please," he whispered, grinding her through yet another orgasm. "Please let me fuck you just one more time."

He was begging and Noah couldn't even be bothered to care because she was going to take this memory – his life, *everything* if he couldn't convince her to at least hesitate.

Killing her was impossible now that he was sure she was his mate. Even though he didn't know her, knew nothing about her – that bond had him all tied up in her until he'd help her slit his throat with a smile on his face rather than see the light leave her eyes.

This was bad. So very, very bad.

"But I like it when you bite me," Harper whispered, sliding a knife into his stomach.

Was that the tart scent of regret, or was he imagining it?

The pain barely registered and Noah couldn't stop fucking her even if he was bleeding out and dying.

Harper twisted the blade and *that* he felt.

"It's a shame really," she murmured, pressing a hand to his forehead. "You're definitely not boring."

Noah felt blackness overtake him and it didn't matter how hard he fought it. She sucked him under until there was nothing left.

6

NOAH

He had a migraine that made no fucking sense, and Noah couldn't figure out what the fuck was wrong with him. Had he really slept on the roof all night long?

The morning sun was above him, making him hot and sweaty.

Liam and Zoe must have had one of their all-nighters or something, because even the veggies were still on the other lounge chair.

Noah checked his phone and saw Morgan and Lily in the call log, so at least that hadn't been a hallucination.

Why had he called Morgan again?

"There you are," Liam said loud enough for all their fucking neighbors to hear.

Noah winced at the sound and rubbed his temples. A migraine was unusual for a wolf, but he'd experienced them before. It was just rare.

"Why is there a witch demanding entrance to our townhouse?" his twin asked, crossing his arms over his chest to study him.

Right, Morgan was going to come here to...to do what?

Why the fuck couldn't he remember anything?

Noah licked his lips and the sweet taste of mangoes exploded on his tongue. It made him instantly hard, and he groaned as the migraine nearly took him out. Both heads were fighting for all the blood in his body, and it was making him feel like he could actually pass out.

"Dude, I know you don't like witches, but she said you called her."

Noah had to get it together or his twin would finally figure out that something was wrong. He'd done such a good job of keeping it from him, and Zoe had been a massive help whether she knew it or not.

What the fuck was going on with him right now? He'd had a bad feeling and then...

Oh, right.

"I wanted her to make sure the wards on the townhouse were secure. We should keep Zoe inside until we're back on the homestead. I'd never forgive myself if something happened to her."

What would happen to her though? Cascade would never attack them in the city. That was the fastest way to get the Council to send their hunters and interfere in pack business. Whatever they decided to do about this territory dispute, no one was going to be pleased, so it was best to just keep them out of it.

If the wards on the townhouse could keep out anything short of a demon, then Zoe would be safe, and that meant his twin would be safe.

"You're hiding from me again." Liam crouched down and waited for Noah to look at him. "What is it you don't want me to know?"

Being a twin was both a blessing and a curse in his opinion. Noah couldn't remember a day he'd ever been separated from Liam except that time they'd been caged and held as collateral to force Shane to obey.

Those had been the worst days of his life, but Noah had stayed alive for Liam. His brother had deserved so much better, and he'd been determined to give it to him.

Something about wolf twins always created a strange anomaly from what the elder wolves had told them. For him and Liam, they could share things like emotions, and thoughts, even as humans.

That wasn't the only thing they shared though.

Unfortunately, the downside was that he couldn't always keep his melancholy feelings from his brother, and Liam didn't need that stress on top of everything else.

"What happened to your shirt?" Liam frowned and plucked at the hole.

Noah felt something lance through his skull as he stared at that hole. "Must have gotten snagged on one of the plants."

Or...something.

He frowned and inspected the tear, wondering how it could be such a perfect slice if he'd torn it on something.

Orange hair and honey-brown eyes flashed through his thoughts and Noah nearly threw up as the memories started assaulting him.

"Fucking hell, dude. Zoe!" Liam was as pale and clammy as Noah felt, his hand pressing to his forehead like he could find out what was going on just from that. "Zoe, get your ass over here right now!"

To her credit, she didn't bitch or moan or complain. It took seconds and suddenly the tiny nurse was crouched in front of him and shining a bright light into his eyes.

"Are they supposed to be glowing?" she asked Liam, pulling up Noah's top lip to see the canines there. "Are shifters supposed to get sweaty like this?"

"Not on their own." Liam tried to force him to lie down, but Noah couldn't stand so many people touching him.

"I'm fine," he tried to assure them, pushing their hands away. "I'm just stressed."

It was definitely not just stress considering how much his stomach ached when he stood. Noah just barely managed to resist touching the spot which was right underneath the hole in his shirt.

Liam didn't believe him, and honestly, Noah knew it was wishful thinking to hope he'd just...ignore all the weird shit. It didn't help that Zoe was just as worried.

"Is there anything I can do?" Liam asked, resting his hand on the back of Noah's neck to help regulate him. "We don't have to live in the city if you can't handle it."

It wouldn't matter where he was, because there was a raven named Harper who had stolen his soul.

Why was he still alive? Shouldn't she have killed him already?

The back of his neck prickled, and he glanced over his shoulder at the building across the street.

He couldn't see her, or smell her, but he could sense her, even with all those charms she wore. Had it really been the mate bond warning him of her presence this whole time?

"Looks like a party," Morgan said as she stepped onto the roof and took in everything with a single sweep of her eyes.

Then she rested that unsettling gaze on him, and Noah shivered when he remembered this witch could do a lot more than scry for the future. She was one of the most powerful witches in her generation, and she could see the past, present, and future with terrifying clarity.

Sometimes he'd swear on his life that she could read minds, not that his life was worth very much these days.

"Your wards could use some updating," Morgan murmured as she slowly walked around the rooftop to examine the plants.

He decided to ignore her and reconsidered the tear in his shirt.

If the raven had stabbed him, where was all the blood? Where was the scent of her on the air? The only thing he had left to remember her by was the taste of her blood on his tongue mixed with mango.

If he didn't have that, Noah would be absolutely positive he'd lost whatever tiny shred of sanity he had left, because it didn't make any fucking sense that a raven contracted to kill him was also his mate.

And she'd chosen not to kill him despite the lack of emotions.

Why was that?

"How are you feeling, Noah?" Morgan asked, coming around until she was standing in front of him, so tiny, just like his mate. "You look pale."

"Just stressed." Noah forced all his thoughts to disappear into nothing as he looked into her eyes and straight up lied. "I'm waiting for my Alpha to call me and tell me how we're going to win this war."

And how he expected Noah to die for this pack.

Morgan grabbed his face and yanked him down as she searched his eyes, her own narrowed in suspicion. "So much death is on your mind, Noah. It's unusually sweet."

Was she able to sense his mate even in the deep recesses of his mind?

Noah closed his eyes and leaned into her cool hand. "Death is always sweet, Morgan. But I have a pack to protect."

Olivia would find her mate even if it cost his life.

He should tell them about the raven, but Noah couldn't bring himself to say her name out loud in case it all turned out to be a figment of his imagination. The memories of her were hazy and the details were escaping him.

What if he'd imagined it all in a very vivid dream? If he said a raven had a contract to kill him, it would only make the others panic and distract them from the real problem at hand.

They needed to destroy Cascade.

Morgan nodded as if she'd heard every thought and for some reason Noah found that comforting.

"Honestly, I'm shocked you like Morgan at all," Liam muttered, wrapping his arm around Zoe. "It took you a long time to warm up to Lily."

That wasn't exactly true.

Noah didn't really care about witches one way or another unless they were making his life a living hell, and Lily had poked her nose in his fucking business every chance she got. She was relentless when it came to finding his mate.

Why she cared so much, he had no idea, but she was a green witch. Setting down roots was kind of her thing.

"Most shifters end up liking me," Morgan whispered like it was somehow a secret. "Let me get to work. You're about to have company anyway."

She released him and his stomach lurched when the doorbell rang. There was no way it could be her, right?

Noah was sprinting down the stairs before he could think twice. The only thought in his head was that if it was her, he had to get there first just in case...

Just in case she really was there to kill him.

Ugh, his head was pounding, and he felt nauseous when he ripped open the front door.

"Oh. It's you." This time, Noah couldn't hide his irritation when he took in the two baby wolves that still hadn't gone through their first shift. "What are you doing here?"

"For fuck's sake, Noah." Liam pushed him aside and grinned at the two humans who managed to survive the bite from the enemy. "Come in. We could really use the help."

"There's a witch upstairs, so don't do anything stupid," Noah warned, watching as they inched by him.

Idiotic, considering he could already smell how much more dominant they were than him. It was annoying how few submissives they'd managed to acquire even with the rash of attacks.

There were so few who had the strength to support a pack.

Zoe and Alexander were the only dominant wolves in the pack who could balance the need for leadership as well as the need for structure and support.

Most dominant wolves that used to be human had too many bad habits from their previous life.

The Alphas and the dominant wolves were there to protect and provide, but they couldn't hold a pack together without their more submissive wolves. The whole thing would fall apart in a heartbeat.

These two were going to have to learn that the hard way, but a war was going to scramble their fragile little brains and ruin any training he could give them.

"Rein it in a little," Liam muttered. "I can smell how pissed off you are and it's filling the whole house."

Noah sighed and looked up at the roof of the condo building across the street, wishing he could see her. It was a shame...

"It's a shame really," she murmured, as she pressed a hand to his forehead. "You're definitely not boring."

The memory of her voice was as sharp and painful as the knife she'd stabbed him with.

When Morgan was done fixing the wards, he was going to ask her to look in his damn head and tell him what was broken, because it felt like his thoughts and feelings had all been tossed into a blender and set to puree.

"Kai is calling me," Zoe grumbled, tossing Liam the phone. "You answer it."

Noah slammed the front door closed and turned to find Morgan standing at the top of the stairs, watching him closely.

"It's Liam," his brother said, answering the phone without hesitation.

"Put me on speaker."

"You two, sit over there," Zoe ordered, pointing at the couch farthest away from Noah. Thank fuck she was more dominant than they were. "Be quiet and just listen. Then we'll figure out what to do with you."

"I see your mate is already getting things in order," Kai said, his tone light and playful despite the obvious tension. "That's good. You're going to need that."

What the ever-loving fuck did that mean?

"I've spoken to Calvin, the Alpha of the Cirque de Nuit Pride, and we came to the decision we think is best considering the situation," Kai said carefully.

For once, Noah didn't watch his brother, he watched Morgan.

The way she sat down on the top stair and propped her elbows on her knees was almost childlike. She rested her chin on her fists and kept her eyes on the phone, but it didn't look like she was actually seeing it.

"I will be officially challenging, Blake Scavage, the Alpha of the Cascade Range Pack for dominance," Kai informed them. "If I win, their pack will join ours, and our territory will expand all the way into Washington."

Dread filled him, and Noah couldn't pinpoint why exactly other than it reminded him too much of the endless stream of Alpha challenges over the last decade.

But even Zoe stayed quiet on this one.

"It's the only way to prevent a slaughter," Kai told them, as if he had to convince himself as well as them. "I was strong enough to beat the last Alpha of the Blue Mountain Pack. Cascade won't be any different."

Except Kai had never wanted to be Alpha. Shane had gone and begged him to take over. Thankfully, Kai was a born Alpha, so he was excellent at his job, but he much preferred the quiet growth and prosperity of running a pack than all this territorial bullshit.

All thoughts of his little raven were gone as Noah considered the various options.

Liam caught his eye and shook his head.

Zoe glared at them both, obviously not pleased to be out of the loop.

He ignored his brother and looked to Morgan – the witch who could see a thousand futures and had promised to help them whenever they needed it.

Morgan nodded once, and Noah realized then that maybe he wasn't so crazy after all if he was right about this witch reading his mind.

"There's another way," Noah started, raising his hand to catch Liam midair. His brother could be so predictable, and he always tried to physically beat him into submission whenever they had a disagreement.

"I'm open to suggestions," Kai admitted. "But nothing that puts the people I swore to protect in harm's way."

Well, that wasn't something Noah could guarantee. But he could promise that it wouldn't cost more than a single life.

"What if I challenged the Alpha?" He wrapped his arms around Liam's neck and held on tight, holding his struggling twin so he wouldn't smack the shit out of him. "I'm the only one without a mate, and it would prove just how incapable of an Alpha he is if he lost to a submissive."

"Is that even possible?" Kai asked, his tone skeptical and disbelieving. "He can smother you with his dominance, Noah. I'm not going to let you do that."

Liam pinched him hard enough to actually hurt

and Noah twisted his nipple in retaliation, earning a sharp yelp that nearly blew out his eardrum.

"About that..." It was time to trust his Alpha, or they'd lose everything. "An Alpha's dominance doesn't work on me."

7

HARPER

"Why are you changing the plan now?" Valentina asked, tossing her phone on the ground and crossing her arms over her chest. "Waiting is only going to increase the complications."

Harper didn't move from her position on the ledge of the roof.

She'd been watching Noah all night and day, and she was positive he remembered her despite how ruthlessly she'd torn every memory of her from his mind.

She hadn't been gentle about it either.

"Our original contract didn't specify potentially having to kill a witch, and not just any witch. She's got connections, not to mention she can see the future better than any Seer an eyrie currently has."

And now her wolfie was trying to sacrifice himself.

Harper wasn't pleased that he would give his life so willingly to anyone but her.

That was almost enough to distract her from the fact that this asshole was her mate of all things.

How ludicrous.

"And that bear shifter is in La Grande now," Valentina admitted, dropping to the ground and crossing her legs with the kind of grace only a raven could accomplish. "He took over the Pack Bar and Grille for the time being. None of the wolves are leaving their property."

"The wards on that land are something else," Harper muttered, considering the witch who looked like she was staring right at her through that bay window. "There's demon magic and something else woven into it that makes it impossible to touch them. We didn't charge enough for this job."

"And now you're acting like you don't want to do it at all." Valentina planted her hands behind her and leaned back, staring up at the cloudless sky. "I thought you wanted freedom."

"I *do* want freedom." Harper bared her teeth at the witch and tried not to flinch when the damn woman *smiled* like she could fucking see her.

Should she tell Valentina about the new complication? Not that she'd ever let some unknown male ever take precedence. No matter how tempting her wolfie was, or how fucking *good* he was at sex, Valentina was her partner, not him.

But then she'd have to tell her how far off the rails she'd fallen by admitting she'd interacted with him.

Still...

"There's something special about one of those wolves," she murmured, sliding a knife out of its sheath – the one she'd stabbed him with. "He can sense me even when I'm wearing all my charms."

"Is that so?" Valentina sounded bored, but there was a spark of interest somewhere in her voice that made Harper smile.

"So, I played a little game with him last night." Harper flipped her knife and wished these wolves would fucking do something already so she could decide what the next step was.

"You're always playing games." Valentina flopped onto the roof, sunning herself like a cat. "What else is new?"

"He knew where I was." She stood and felt the wind whip around her, practically pushing her off the rooftop. Harper didn't like how the witch's eyes kept following her. "It turns out the mate bond was overriding all my magic, rendering it useless."

"The mate bond?" Suddenly that sharp voice was right behind her, and Harper half-expected the other raven to shove her off the edge. "Interesting. Are you sure?"

Her shoulder was still sore, but it had felt so good it was kind of hard to be annoyed by it.

"He went feral," Harper admitted, smiling at the memory of those silver eyes looking up at her while he suffocated on her pussy. Noah certainly hadn't let that stop him from giving her the best head she'd ever had. "I had to steal his memories, but it seems like he's remembered anyway."

"This is going to be a problem." Valentina watched the house with her for a good ten minutes in silence. "We should just cancel the contract. A submissive is going to challenge Blake anyway. They won't need us to kill the wolves if they really go through with that asinine plan. If anything, Cascade will short us the second half of their payment."

It was interesting that Valentina was so willing to drop it considering she was in the same boat as Harper.

"Why are you fine abandoning this contract?" Harper turned to study the other raven even knowing her emotionless face would tell her nothing. Her aura was always a soothing violet that meant the assassin was still calmer than ever despite the change.

"You know I don't like killing witches. We've always gotten along with them, and our relationship is symbiotic. They're the only ones allowed in our eyries."

Harper had given up everything except her training and a partnership. Valentina had held onto the love for witches that ravens couldn't seem to help. It was kind of cute, but it wasn't something she'd say out loud unless she wanted to get stabbed.

"And there are always people that need killing." Valentina shrugged and studied Harper from head to toe. "If you want to play with your wolf, killing him would make that impossible, no?"

She tilted her head and tried to understand why Valentina would care.

"The whole reason we left our Collectives, and the rule of the Enclave, was so we could have the freedom to choose what we do with our lives," Valentina reminded her. "That means canceling a contract if something feels off, or if the situation unexpectedly changes. That witch down there? She's clearly connected to the kind of people who could kill us without even trying if she got demons to protect their land. I'm not interested in ruining my future because a bunch of wolves got greedy. Are you?"

"And if the Cascade Alpha tries to force the matter?" Harper turned back to the townhouse and wondered what made Noah think he could take on someone like Blake. That dominance had been suffocating, even if it had zero effect on her.

It had left a bad taste, and her wolfie was one of the most submissive in his own pack. How would he manage it long enough to challenge him?

"Our contract states we can cancel if the situation

is not what was previously agreed upon and he must forgo the deposit. If he tries to force the matter..." Valentina shrugged a shoulder. "We kill him."

That would certainly be more interesting, now wouldn't it?

"What do you want to do then?" Not that she wanted a mate or anything, but she couldn't deny that her mouth watered just imagining what it would be like to fuck him again.

Maybe this time she'd even let him kiss her.

Valentina jumped up on the ledge beside her and grinned. "Do you want to play a game?"

"Always." Harper couldn't help but join her. This was why she'd agreed to work with Valentina after all. "What did you have in mind?"

"Let's find out what your little wolf is truly capable of and figure out what that witch has to do with it all. She can clearly See us, and I want to know why she hasn't said anything."

Valentina propped her elbow on Harper's shoulder and considered the woman staring at them with this pretty pink glow in her eyes – evidence of just how powerful she was.

"Then we'll decide what to do about Cascade. They hid the full truth from us, and you know how I feel about that."

Harper felt her grin sharpen. She did know. Valentina was ruthless when it came to lies and half-truths. No one *ever* lied to her, even by omission, and got away with it.

No, the raven would leave a warning in the form of a body and move on like nothing happened.

There were always people to kill and money to make. Another couple of weeks wouldn't bring their Collectives down on them just yet.

Plus, one of these wolves seemed to be her mate?

Cascade's contract was as good as dead, but the details...the devil was always in the details, and that was what made the game so interesting.

"Wanna bet on who's going to win?" she asked, slipping an arm around Valentina's waist so she could feel the steady rhythm of her heart beating in tandem with her own.

"I'm not stupid enough to bet against you," Valentina chuckled. She even winked at the witch. "We're going to pick a side and light a match. Then we'll watch the other one burn. Didn't they used to say it only took two ravens to destroy an empire?"

"It's been a long time since we've reminded them of that." Harper rested her head on Valentina's arm and couldn't wait for the sun to set. "Do you want to go watch Cascade, or La Grande?"

"I'll take Cascade and you deal with Blue Mountain. Then we'll have the most up-to-date intel. Although, I imagine that witch could give us even better intel if you could charm her into giving it to us."

"I can charm anyone and anything if I feel like it." Telling Valentina had been the right choice. She'd just have to make sure nothing happened to her because of this decision.

If her Collective tried to come after Valentina, Harper would make sure that entire Administration was replaced before they stole her partner.

Even without emotions, she'd always been possessive.

And that wolf was *hers*.

Crouched on his windowsill, she watched him sleep with her arms wrapped around her legs.

The window was open, and March was still fucking freezing at night, but this idiot wolf liked to sleep with it open even when winter still had a death grip on the city.

Harper wondered if he'd left it open for her, or if this was just how he liked to sleep.

The moment she slipped the charms from around her neck, Noah rolled over so he was facing her, still asleep, and Harper got an eyeful of those massive pecs of his. They were all squished together and practically begging for her to shove her face between them.

It was weird how much she liked it when his brother had the exact same body, but it didn't get the same physical reaction out of her. Harper wondered why that was.

They were identical on the outside, and technically she didn't give a shit about the inside, not when she had no emotions or empathy.

She slid off the ledge and the moment the toe of her boot touched the floor, Noah's eyes snapped open.

They were the same bright silver as the crescent moon above her.

"Finally going to kill me?" he murmured, blinking as a smile slowly spread across his face.

Bless the Morrigan for making her mate so fucking beautiful. It certainly made the entire concept less disgusting.

Harper was across the room before he finished blinking. "I haven't decided."

"What changed your mind?" Noah slid an arm around her waist and pulled her closer so he could press his face against her stomach. "You smell exactly like I remember."

Tossing her charms on his nightstand felt like a mistake, but he could sense her even with the magic, so there was just no point in bothering with it – not when all it took to make him feral was the taste of her.

"It's troublesome you keep remembering that I exist." She pushed his hair out of his face, and he grumbled when it shoved him off of her. "What makes you so special, wolfie?"

He grinned up at her like an idiot, eyes glowing like the otherworldly creature he was. "I was born defective."

Interesting.

"Is that why you challenged an Alpha?" She climbed up into his bed until she was straddling him, curious what his reason for that was.

"No shoes or clothes in my bed." Noah stared up at her like she might just be a dream, but one he had no plans of waking up from. "Maybe I'll tell you when you're riding me."

Harper laughed, enjoying the fact that he didn't seem to care *how* she rode him as long as he was inside her.

A snap of her fingers activated the charm stitched into her skin and every scrap of clothing she had on, as well as her boots and knives, simply disappeared.

It had been a totally stupid vanity charm that she'd spent way too much money on, but it was nice to know she'd always have clothes even if she shifted back and forth faster than any mortal could possibly follow.

And it had the exact effect on Noah she'd been anticipating.

His entire body stiffened, and claws erupted from his fingertips at the same time that his canines elongated. Black hair covered his eyes, but the silver shone through like the stars in a night sky.

"Why aren't you afraid of me?" she asked, shifting so she could move the blanket out of the way.

The moment her skin touched his, it was like every ache and pain she didn't know she had disappeared.

"I've been courting death for most of my life," Noah confessed, his claws digging into her thighs. "It seems fitting that my mate would be death herself. Don't you think?"

Honestly, Harper had no idea what to think about that.

All she could do was stare at him as she tried to understand why he didn't seem to care even a little bit that she was supposed to kill him. Harper hadn't given him a shred of hope that he might live either.

No, this wolf didn't seem to care about that at all.

"Is that why you're challenging an Alpha?"

"Aw, do you care if I live or die, little raven?" Noah smirked up at her and she wanted to wipe that shit right off his face by making him whimper and cry.

Or he could beg. She'd liked that.

"Your life and death are *mine*," she reminded him, shifting her weight so his massive, hard cock was nestled between her thighs and pressed right against her slick center. "You're not allowed to give it to someone else."

"Possessive," Noah teased, thrusting up to slide through the wetness pooling between them. "I like it."

"You're an idiot," she hissed, leaning forward until

her nose was pressed to his. Their lips were close enough it would be too easy to kiss him, but he hadn't earned that. "You can't win against an Alpha, and you certainly can't win against me."

"I'm already winning." Noah gripped her waist tight enough to bruise and pulled her up the length of him before slowly pushing her back down.

The pressure was so good her thighs were already shaking.

How the fuck did he do that?

"Because you're in my bed, totally naked. You want to fuck me again, don't you?" What a fucking brat. Harper didn't think she'd ever met a submissive so fucking sassy and confident. "Tell me you want to fuck me again, little raven. I promise I'll make it worth delaying my death."

She wasn't originally going to tell him about the change in plans, but maybe...maybe if he earned it, she'd give him that too.

"You don't care if I kill you after?" she asked, settling both hands on his chest so she could squeeze those luscious pecs.

"I'd die happy as long as I get to taste you one more time," he said, the words practically reverent. "Though I'd prefer if you didn't kill me, only because then I could fuck you for the rest of my life – however long or short that might be."

"And your brother?" She tapped his nose and

wiggled her hips, enjoying the sharp hiss of pleasure mixed with the ache he had to be feeling.

"That's my hard limit," Noah admitted. "Just leave him out of this."

So, if they decided to go through with the contract to Cascade, she'd have to kill Noah first.

Harper froze as she tried to figure out why she would even care about that.

Her emotions were off, weren't they?

There was a frantic moment where she wasn't sure, but no, that switch was still off.

Strange that a wolf could make her question her own training, even if he did happen to be her mate.

Harper studied his aura and noticed that it was a lighter blue than the day before, even if it was still nice and dark. It reminded her of sapphires and blue velvet. It was soft, but deep enough to drown in.

He'd probably lived like this his whole life too.

Even while he waited for her to make her choice, Noah was constantly moving her against his cock, creating a gentle friction that kept building and building until he had her right on the edge of an orgasm, but he never quite let her reach the pinnacle.

Crafty *and* bratty, it seemed.

Harper grinned down at him, letting the ruby red shine through. "Wanna play a game with me, wolfie?"

8

HARPER

"A game?" Noah asked, his eyes focused on the place where her body met his. The constant slip and slide of him against her was an exquisite kind of torture that Harper couldn't quite bring herself to rid the world of just yet. "What kind of game?"

Her fingers wrapped around his throat and Noah lifted his chin, giving her better access even knowing how easy it would be for her to drag a knife across the soft skin, or snap it too fast for him to stop her.

"Convince me that it would be a better choice for me to let you live," she murmured, running her thumb along the column of his throat. "And I'll cancel my contract."

Noah paused, his silver eyes lifting to study her ruby ones. "Why would you do that? Isn't it dangerous?"

"That's my business, not yours." She tapped his nose like she would a naughty hatchling and tried to ignore just how plump and delicious his lips looked.

Harper sat back and pinched his nipples as she waited for his response, enjoying his sharp inhale of pain.

Noah was too good at this, and her instincts were warning her that she was playing a dangerous game with him, one that was far more unforgiving than the one she was playing with Cascade.

"Would you stay with me?" Noah asked, flipping her over before she could stop him. The way he caged her against the mattress made Harper uncomfortable. "If I could convince you, would I be yours and you'd be mine?"

The earnest words eased some of her discomfort and Harper studied this wolf and his aura closely. "I can't love you, Noah. If I stayed, I'd never love you back."

His slow smile would have been terrifying if she could feel anything at all, but Harper just felt a warning in her gut.

This was not a normal reaction. He should be even more depressed than before.

"But you'd be with me?" he asked, burying his nose in her neck and inhaling deeply.

"You don't care that your mate could abandon you at any moment without a care in the world, the very second she got bored with you?" Harper asked, wondering if he was right in the head.

"Why would I care?" Noah nipped the spot he seemed obsessed with and readjusted his hips, so the tip of his cock was pressed right against her entrance. "I'll love you enough for the both of us. You can't stop me from doing that. And if you leave, I'll just follow you around like a lost puppy. It seems like something you'd be into anyways."

Annoying that he was right about that.

Harper pushed him back so she could have more room to breathe – more room to *think*.

"That wasn't the game I suggested."

"But you didn't say it was off the table." Noah sat back on his heels and dragged her closer, admiring her while she lay there beneath him. "Just be with me, Harper. I don't need anything else."

She rolled her eyes, suddenly no longer in the mood. "Says the wolf who challenged an Alpha like a fucking idiot."

His massive hand pressed down on her chest when she tried to get up, and Harper felt her eyes widen in surprise when she realized just how strong he was.

This wolf was so much stronger than her.

But he wasn't faster.

Before he'd finished blinking, she'd flipped him onto *his* back, and then Harper pressed the tips of her fingers into the pressure points that would make him lose consciousness if she didn't let go in time.

Noah didn't look the least bit surprised or upset. In fact, his aura shifted with the pressure on his throat, making that navy blue edge into a strange purple-pink. If she wasn't sure about how much he liked it, the deep groan and thrust of his hips told her enough.

This was turning him on even more, and Harper honestly hadn't thought that was possible.

"Please," he begged, eyes wild and desperate. "Ride me, Harper. I need you."

She increased the pressure on his throat, and Noah whimpered, thrusting up again. The way his cock leaked told her he was so fucking close she might just get him to come without much provocation at all.

Keeping track of the way his pulse slowed, she watched him closely, squeezing his throat again. Noah's chest heaved as he tried to breathe, but she wasn't cutting off his air supply. She was stopping the flow of blood to his brain while allowing him only small sips of air to prolong the experience.

He tried to move, his hands gripping her arms as he silently begged, his lips moving as he tried to say *please* over and over and over.

Right before he lost consciousness, she loosened her hold, letting the blood flow to his brain for a few seconds before cutting it off again.

Noah thrashed beneath her, trying to get inside

her, but she straddled him, letting it rub against her instead. It was like riding a bucking bronco, but Harper held on to him like it was her job.

His desperation was mesmerizing.

How could he feel all this for her?

"You're losing your mind over a fabrication," she murmured, watching his eyes roll back into his head when she loosened her grip again, but her other hand on his chest kept him willingly pinned.

Harper wasn't an idiot. This wolf could put up a real fight if he wanted to, but the cruel hope that she might give him the chance and finally sheathe his cock and ride him into oblivion... it was something he didn't dare ruin.

"The mate bond is nothing but magic and biology," she reminded him, sliding her hand down his chest as she increased the pressure on his throat again. "It's telling your body that you can't live without me despite how ridiculous and impossible our situation is. It's addling your mind and telling you I'm the only one who can ever complete you – *me*, the one who will bring you more death than you could ever imagine."

Gently, she wrapped her hand around his cock, spreading the ridiculous amount of precum over the soft skin until she could hear squelching as she slid her hand down the length of him.

"Please, please," Noah begged, thrusting into her

hand. "I don't care. I don't *care*, I just want you—*need* you. *Please*."

His sharp claws dug into her thighs and drew blood, but Harper didn't stop him. She didn't hurry either, stroking upward and over the tip, smiling slightly at how much precum gushed out when she loosened her hold on his throat completely, letting the blood rush to his head.

Noah was clearly lightheaded and just shy of feral as he moaned, thrusting in time with her movements when she didn't once stop stroking him. Harper felt his cock harden even more, and she was ready to watch him climax.

She wanted to see him fall apart for her, but it didn't happen.

Instead, he whimpered like he was in pain, those silver eyes locking onto hers. "Please, I need to be inside you."

Tilting her head, she was surprised to find he could hold back like this considering how feral he was. "You can climax as many times as you want," she told him, stroking harder and faster. "Not all of them have to be inside of me."

"*Harper*," the sharp tone and the growl behind her name told her the wolf inside him was so close to the surface that she was playing a *very* dangerous game indeed. "I was made for you. Let me prove it."

She highly doubted that.

Instead, she gripped him so hard around the throat that he couldn't breathe at all and stroked his huge cock with the same amount of pressure. "You can come for me, or you can pass out before you do, but you'll wake up alone if you don't come. Your choice, Noah."

Another whimper nearly destroyed her control, but she was going to see him do what *she* wanted first, or she'd simply leave.

The stubborn brat nearly lost consciousness as she twisted and pumped him, but Noah snarled at the last minute, his claws digging deeper into her thighs, and the cum that spurted from his cock painted his chest in pretty white ribbons.

It kept coming and Harper stroked him through it, releasing his throat as she took as much of that cum from him as she could.

She was going to fuck his brains out tonight.

There was no rush when they were both shifters. She had all night and she planned to savor every fucking minute.

"The mate bond is real, just like all magic is real," she murmured, licking her lips when he started shaking because she wouldn't stop stroking him, begging her to *stop* when another gush of cum covered her hand. "But would you have chosen me without magic convincing you I was the answer to all your problems?"

Noah gripped her wrist, trying to pull her off of

him, but the orgasm had made him weak. "Harper, *please*."

"Do you even know what you're asking me for anymore?" She grinned and scooted down, ignoring just how fucking wet and achy she was. Torturing him was so much more fun than getting off. "I've been contracted to kill you, Noah. I've been contracted to assassinate your entire pack, including your twin and his pretty little mate."

Finally, something in his eyes flickered, telling her he was actually hearing what she was saying even if it hadn't quite registered yet.

Then she licked the cum from the tip of his cock and he groaned, throwing his head back. Harper licked him clean, dragging her fingers through the cum on his chest to paint mindless patterns.

"I feel nothing for your pack, or for you," she said, leaning down to lick the cum from his stomach.

Harper stuck her tongue out and gripped his jaw hard enough his eyes popped open. Noah couldn't stop staring at the white pool in her mouth as she undulated her tongue, letting it slip out of her mouth and down her chin.

"You taste good, puppy. I wasn't expecting that," she said after swallowing. "The only reason you're even alive is because you taste delicious and feel even better."

Gently, she stroked him as she licked the rest of his

cum from his chest, not that it really mattered. It wasn't like she could get pregnant anyway. She just wanted him inside *her* for once.

"Why do you want someone who can't love you?" she asked once he was all clean. "Are you a masochist?"

He gripped her face and yanked her up. "*Yes.*"

Oh, sweet Morrigan, that confession nearly shattered what was left of her restraint.

"I could deny the mate bond right now, and mean it," she teased, pulling out of his grip.

She resettled between his legs and watched him as she licked up the column of his cock.

The way he trembled beneath her was intoxicating.

"You could, but you haven't yet," Noah gritted out, shaking when she sucked him into her mouth. "Why not? It would be so easy. Then you wouldn't have to hear me beg like some pathetic asshole."

His aura was darkening again, and she didn't respond as she sucked him like her life depended on it.

Harper bobbed her head up and down as she knelt between his legs, sucking and stroking with her hand. He hit the back of her throat over and over, too damn big for his own good, but she relaxed as much as she could, forcing him down until her nose brushed against his stomach.

It made her want to gag, but she fought the sensation because of the way he kept whispering *oh, fuck* over and over. It was almost enough to make her come. Harper looked up and held his gaze as she slid her free hand down his leg.

She started moving again, licking him all over just to make him fucking crazy. The taste of his precum was salty and sweet, like salted watermelon.

Just the thought had her mouth watering and she saw the moment he realized what she was doing. Harper watched him zero in on her hand like the predator he was when she started rubbing her clit, sucking him again with the same rhythm he could see with his very own eyes.

That was all it took for him to lose it all over again.

Cum filled her mouth as a strangled sound of both pleasure and pain left him. It was too much even though she tried to swallow it all. His cum leaked from the corners of her mouth and Noah started shaking like a leaf as he watched with wide eyes.

He was shaking *bad*, trying to stop her when she kept sucking, her own pleasure forgotten as she watched him mutter nonsense in between the whimpering and begging.

This was almost better than when he'd eaten her out like she was the sweetest dessert.

"Stop, please stop, Harper—I can't—*Harper*."

More cum gushed into her mouth, but it wasn't a real orgasm despite the pained groan. She'd just managed to prolong it all until he gave her everything she wanted.

"You're doing this on purpose," he gasped, nothing but a quivering mess beneath her. "Can't prove I'm worth keeping if you—if you..."

She finally stopped because he was about to actually pass out. Grinning, she licked the cum that had escaped her mouth from her hand and his body, waiting for him to come down from the high just a little.

"Can't prove it if you don't let me," he finally finished, his voice thick and guttural, echoing with the sound of his wolf.

Harper wanted to push him all the way over until he was feral and fighting her for control. She wanted him to fuck her like he meant it, *pissed* that she'd turned him into a mess before he could prove shit.

"You're just scared," he muttered, eyes closing when she slid her own juices over his cock, surprised he could come so much without once softening.

Shifter libido never disappointed, but this was something else entirely.

"You're scared you're going to like it too much," Noah told her, groaning when she climbed up his body to tease his nipples.

The way his chest heaved when she licked one made those glorious pecs jiggle and it was distracting enough she didn't punish him for insinuating she'd be scared of *anything*, let alone him.

Harper pinched the one she'd licked and went for the other, sucking it into her mouth hard.

Noah's body was boneless, and he didn't have the strength to do anything other than let her feast on him. He was still shaking, mindless from all the overstimulation.

One more time. She'd make him come one more time, and then she'd ride him. Harper wanted to know why he'd do something as stupid as challenging an Alpha after all.

Shoving his pecs together, she sat back and admired them before pinching both nipples this time.

"Say something, dammit." Noah's hands slid up her thighs, smearing the blood across her skin from the already healed wounds.

"*Something.*" Harper giggled when he snarled at her, eyes slitted in irritation. "What do you want me to say?"

"Why haven't you rejected the mate bond?" he asked, watching her play with his giant biddies, a small smile playing on his lips. "It would make things easier for you, right?"

She tilted her head and roughly pinched his nipples again and he hissed in pain, lurching up to a sitting position.

His arm went around her waist, and she could feel

how hard he still was against her clit. It made her whole fucking pussy clench, but Harper ignored it as she considered him.

"Nothing about this is easy," she admitted, wriggling against him. She adored the way his eyes slid closed at the sensation. "I get bored easily, and so far, you've kept me entertained longer than anyone else I've fucked before. It seems like a waste to let you go so soon."

"Let me prove it," he murmured, leaning closer to rub his nose along her jaw, pressing a kiss where her jaw met her throat. "Let me prove I can keep you entertained for the rest of my life."

His teeth scraped upward, and she shivered, considering if she wanted to do that, or if she wanted to follow through with her original plan to make him orgasm again first.

Harper liked the way his hands felt on her skin, and his teeth were sharp. She liked it so much she lost herself in the sensation.

Eyes closing, she enjoyed his soft touches, and contemplated.

This puppy was so *very* dangerous.

Before she could snap out of it, Noah pressed his lips to hers, stealing a kiss.

Oh, she was *definitely* going to kill him now.

9

NOAH

There was no one in the world like Harper. Noah was pretty sure there was no one in the whole fucking *universe* like her either.

It didn't matter how many realms there were of all the various realities and timelines. *This* Harper was a fucking menace, and she played his body like she knew every teeny tiny little thing about it.

Noah had never lost his senses quite like this before. He'd never been so far gone that he didn't even have the strength to get her to stop.

Not that he really wanted her to stop.

And somehow she knew that too.

The way she watched him, the masterful way she used breath play to force him into orgasm after orgasm...

Noah was ready to get down on his knees—

actually, no. He was ready to bare his throat *and* soul. If she cared enough to ask him, he'd tell her he'd already accepted the mate bond somewhere after the third orgasm she'd forced on him.

Wait...he was pretty sure it was when she'd forced him to see the cum on her tongue and the way she'd let it drip right back onto his cock just so she could lick it off *again*.

Kinky fucking bitch.

Noah was head over heels in love with her no matter how stupid that was.

If she decided to leave at dawn and never return, he'd spend the rest of his life searching for her. Then, if he managed to find her, he'd follow her to the ends of the Earth and beyond just like he'd promised.

But...if she rejected the mate bond and meant it...

Noah tasted himself on her lips. He tasted her fury too, but he didn't stop kissing her.

For whatever reason, Harper had been totally fine swallowing him—licking him clean, and generally making a sexy nuisance of herself, but the moment he did something as innocent as kissing her, he could smell the urge to kill that was nearly as strong as the desire coating her.

Where she got the knife, he didn't know and didn't care. Noah licked her lips one last time, ignoring the blade slicing into his skin as he leaned forward to get one last taste.

Might as well steal it before she took his life.

She owed him that much at least.

"I didn't give you permission to kiss me," she hissed, digging the point of her blade into the soft, fleshy part under his chin.

This blade didn't smell like steel. No, it was salted silver if his nose was right, and Noah's nose was rarely ever wrong.

"You mean it this time," he murmured, taking her wrist and bringing the knife up. Noah licked the blade, feeling his tongue burn thanks to the silver. It barely registered thanks to all the endorphins she'd flooded his stupid fucking brain with.

"I *always* mean it," Harper snapped, pulling back so she didn't slice the tip of his tongue off.

"This blade is silver though," he stated, sucking the blood from his tongue with half-lidded eyes.

He was so drunk off her he was barely on this planet. It felt like he was going to float away thanks to the absolute bliss she'd given him.

But he was still hard, still desperate to fill her.

It just didn't feel like enough no matter how many times he'd come. Noah still hadn't been able to sheathe himself inside her and feel that warmth again. He hadn't been able to taste her pleasure or watch her quiver beneath him.

Instead, she'd been the one to watch him fall apart over and over.

Noah might be embarrassed about it if she didn't seem so fucking pleased with herself.

And it wasn't like he couldn't still follow through with his promise – it might just kill him though...

There was no better way to go, in his opinion.

"Last time you stabbed me with a mundane blade – nothing but steel." He licked her knife again, watching her face for those tiny little reactions he doubted she knew he could see. "This time, you want the pain to linger."

"I don't like kissing," she told him, tossing the blade to the floor.

Harper was faster than the devil, and Noah suddenly found his tongue trapped between her finger and thumb. The way she watched it slowly heal made him wonder if she was truly as emotionless as she claimed.

It wasn't the first time she'd been peeved he was so reckless with his life, and Noah wondered why that was. He really didn't think it was just because she had some weird sense of ownership over his life and death thanks to the assassination contract.

"Maybe you just haven't been kissed by the right person," he murmured, sliding his hands down her back and over that perfect ass.

It was thick and curvy, but not soft at all. He could feel the muscle and knew she was the real deal. This was a *raven assassin* – the same thing that had nearly cost him, his twin, Shane, and then his mate, Bonnie, their lives.

"I hate ravens," he confessed, sliding a hand between her ass cheeks.

Dear fucking god, she was so wet she was dripping. It had leaked down while she'd been sucking him off, covering her pussy and ass until it was drenched and ready.

"One of your brethren nearly killed my twin because he was stupid." Noah slid his fingers between her folds and closed his eyes at the luscious sensation. "A cruel Alpha captured him. He thought he was too good for a partner and was working solo. This Alpha had a witch on the payroll. It was too easy to put a leash on the raven and turn him into a pet."

Harper was frozen even though she was straddling him, all wet and ready. It was crazy what a lack of emotions could accomplish when it came to restraint.

Noah opened his eyes to find hers glowing the same ruby red as the assholes who'd tried to kill Bonnie.

"Our Alpha at the time locked Liam and me in separate cages," he explained, sliding two fingers inside her. "You see, our lives mattered to the Second. It kept him from pushing the Alpha to release that raven, because if he tried again, he wouldn't walk away with a broken leg and a witch who forced him to heal like a human. He'd have to watch Liam and me die by his raven's hands."

The ruby red in Harper's eyes seemed both brighter and darker at the same time. The red was so dark it was nearly black, but it lit up the whole fucking room and painted it in blood.

"Eventually, the Alpha got bored and killed that raven," Noah admitted, sliding his fingers out of her. The way her breath caught nearly had him begging her all over again, but she needed to understand. "A few years later, the family of that raven tried to call in their blood debt."

Her breath caught again when he moved them both, pulling her against his chest and along the entire length of his cock.

"Those ravens tried to kill Shane's mate – to make sure he understood what it felt like to lose someone important to him." She was so wet he slid right in, but *fuck,* she was tight.

They both gasped when the walls of her pussy clamped around him, nearly making him come on the spot.

What the fuck was his deal with this girl? It was like he was ready to bust every time she touched him, and his body seemed content to do it over and over again until he passed out from overstimulation and dehydration.

It was notoriously difficult for a shifter to lose

consciousness from either of those things thanks to their healing, but this kinky little bitch nearly had him there more than a few times now.

"We killed them all," he whispered into her ear, dropping his head and resting his chin on her shoulder. "Now we owe the Salem eyrie a blood debt. Did you know that?"

She didn't say anything when he bit down on her shoulder, careful not to break the skin this time. Harper held so still he knew she was on the edge of losing her careful, perfect control.

Noah scraped his sharp canines along her shoulder and up her neck, forcing himself not to move inside of her. If she wanted friction, she could take it for herself, because he was quite happy just being inside her.

"Are you part of the Salem eyrie?" he asked, brushing his lips across the line of her jaw.

She was so pissed she was practically vibrating in his arms, but he didn't stop.

Noah was going to steal another kiss before she killed him, and there was nothing she could do about it.

"I'm not part of *any* eyrie," she snapped, hissing in a breath when he lightly bit her chin. "I took this job because I wanted to, not because the Enclave demanded it."

Good to know.

Noah gripped her ass with both hands and squeezed, his long fingers nearly reaching her back entrance. "Well, I suppose that's better than the alternative."

Right when she was about to protest, he flexed his fingers and pressed her as close as possible. Noah slid his tongue between her lips and kissed her again before she could stop him.

Her lips were so soft – such a contrast to everything she was. Noah had no idea what she would be like with emotions, but he kind of hoped she'd be just as unhinged and unremorseful as she was now.

The taste of her mouth was salty thanks to all his cum, but she was still exotic and sweet. Harper tasted like something he'd only ever dreamt about.

Freedom.

For whatever reason, she didn't try to gut him this time. Harper even wrapped her arms around his neck and sighed into him, opening her mouth wider to let him take whatever he wanted.

Such a contrast. It had his head spinning and Noah got lost in her.

Nothing else existed.

"You scared?" he whispered against her lips, smirking when her nails ripped the skin on his shoulders open.

Noah leaned back and admired her. The sight of her straddling him made his dick flex inside her and Harper clenched around him in response.

It was almost more than he could resist, but she'd

taken so many orgasms from him, he was more than happy to lie there and let her do the work for whatever it was she wanted.

He didn't need to come again, but he definitely needed to have her climax enough times she couldn't even remember she was supposed to steal his memories yet again.

"Speechless?" he asked, running his nails gently over her thighs. "I'm shocked."

"I'm simply trying to decide if I should make you cry this time around," she said, lifting her body with those thick, strong thighs before dropping mercilessly back down on him.

Noah's claws dug into her skin again and the scent of her blood was almost good enough to eat. He wanted to devour her the way she was slowly devouring him, but first he had to convince her he wasn't boring.

"You said it was the Salem eyrie?" she asked, doing the same fucking thing, dropping onto him in such a way he hit deep and she fucking clenched him so hard he saw stars.

There was no way he could stay sane through this torture. She was driving him higher and higher, all the while looking as cool as a cucumber and totally unaffected.

"Mhm." He lifted his hips, eyes half-mast as he considered what might get her to break. "Ride me, little raven. Ride me hard and I'll tell you anything you want to know."

"Can you stay conscious through it?" she teased, hips slowly moving as she started gyrating above him.

Perfection.

The torture was exquisite, and he never wanted it to end.

Noah was still so fucking sensitive he didn't think it would take much for her to get him to come all over again like a fucking child who'd never had his dick touched.

Whether she wanted to attribute all this to the fake lust the mate bond created or not, it didn't matter. Noah had never been like this with anyone before. He'd barely ever been interested in more than one round, and no one had ever gotten him to come like she had.

There was *nothing* he wouldn't do to keep her.

Harper slowly rode him, her hands resting on his pecs.

She loved his chest, and Noah almost laughed when she squeezed the muscles again, but she slammed down on him like she knew he was laughing at her, pulling a guttural moan from him that was more wolf than human.

At some point, he'd completely lose his mind. Did she understand what that meant?

"Be careful," he managed, licking his canines as he

watched her ride him – slow and lazy. "Push me too much and I won't be able to stop. Even if you really mean it—even if you stab me. I'd fuck you to death and hate myself for it, but I still wouldn't stop."

Harper licked her lips and it almost seemed like the idea was exactly what she wanted from him. "Duly noted, puppy. But I don't know if you've noticed...I've been hoping for that."

That was almost enough to tip him right over the edge.

Noah held impossibly still and closed his eyes. It took everything he had to pretend he couldn't smell her blood, the mate bond, or the scent of mangoes between her legs.

His canines pricked his lips and he inhaled slowly, trying to remind his wolf that she wouldn't like a half-shifted creature pounding into her. If they wanted any chance of convincing her to stay, he needed to stay mostly sane.

"What makes you think you can challenge the Alpha of Cascade and win?" Harper demanded, leaning forward so her lips brushed against his. "You're a submissive wolf. He will have you kneeling before the fight truly begins, and then he will rip your head from your shoulders."

"My death has been promised to you," Noah murmured, opening his eyes just to find her tits in his face.

He bit down before he could stop himself, sucking her nipple into his mouth through his teeth.

She let out a little screech, but Harper arched into him instead of pulling away.

Pressing her into his face, Noah turned his head and sank his teeth into her other tit, relishing in the taste of her blood and desire and the way she fucking pulsed around him in response to every suck on her soft flesh.

"I'd never let the Alpha kill me," he promised, nuzzling his face between her breasts. "Only you can kill me, Harper. I'd die happy at your hands."

"That doesn't explain why you think it's even possible," she snapped, threading her fingers through his hair and yanking back so he was forced to look at her. "You're submissive."

Noah grinned up at her, licking her blood from his teeth. "I was born defective, pretty little assassin. I may be submissive, but the Alpha command doesn't work on me. He can demand I drop to my knees until he's blue in the face. All I have to do is rip his throat out while he's too stunned to stop me."

Her eyes shifted from that ruby red glow to the gorgeous honey brown as she took that in. "How is that possible? You're a wolf shifter."

Noah was done talking about this. "How are *you* possible?" he asked, sitting back up and shifting his weight until he was kneeling on the bed, his hands gripping her ass to keep her in place.

He was hard enough that even if he let go, she wouldn't go anywhere, but Noah liked the excuse to fondle her.

"*Noah.*" Harper sounded like she was going to argue with him about something she couldn't possibly understand, but this time, he wasn't having it.

"It's my turn," he told her.

Then he snagged her bottom lip between his teeth and pulled her closer.

Harper's orange hair had silver highlights under the moonlight and Noah didn't dare blink when she miraculously didn't fight this.

Was she going to let him kiss her again?

Releasing her lip, he squeezed her ass, pulling up and then down to start up that delicious friction again.

Her little moan of pleasure told him he was doing a good job even if she was still stuck on what he'd told her.

Noah slid his hands up her sides and he watched her closely, breathing in every scent from her he could.

No emotions at all.

It was fucking bizarre, but he couldn't say he hated it.

"So perfect," he murmured, licking her chin playfully. "Stay with me until dawn?"

A few hours were nothing compared to forever, but

he was going to steal that too, along with the kisses she supposedly hated.

"Dawn," Harper agreed, rolling her hips. "I can stay until then. Don't make me regret it, puppy."

He grinned at that.

She had no fucking idea what she'd just agreed to, but he was going to show her until the sun was shining through his window and she was begging him to stop.

Noah flipped her onto her back so fast, she gasped, looking up at him with wide eyes. "Don't worry, Mistress Raven. I'll make you wish dawn would never come."

10

NOAH

Just like the last time he'd put her on her back, Harper tensed up. Her hands were on his shoulders like she was ready to push him back at any second and the prick of her sharp nails were a warning.

Noah searched her eyes, watching the ruby red flicker in and out like she was nervous. It was disconcerting because he didn't scent a drop of anxiety or nerves on her.

"I'm not done asking you about the Alpha," she told him, sounding less angry than she probably wanted. "Aren't I supposed to ride you for information?"

Noah smiled, glad to see that the intense curiosity of ravens wasn't just a rumor. She'd fixated on something she wanted – badly enough she was letting him take over to some degree.

"I changed my mind," Noah drawled, slowly pulling out of her. "I want you like this while you ask me all your questions."

Her eyes narrowed, but she didn't argue with him as he slowly slid back inside of her. Once he was fully sheathed, he ground against her, watching her lips part as he stimulated everything he could touch.

Harper was close, he could feel it in the way she pulsed around him faster and faster even though she didn't move with him.

What was she waiting for?

He dipped his head and licked both his bite marks on her tits, seeing that they'd already started healing. It was weird that ravens didn't heal as fast as wolves, but it was still closing before his very eyes.

Why did she keep letting him claim her?

Noah had done it so many times now without ever once asking her. It was technically a violation and he wanted to hate himself for not caring if she consented to it or not, but...

Wouldn't she have just gutted him if she didn't want it?

Harper liked the feel of his teeth. Her reaction when he bit the healing bite mark again was so good he couldn't help but growl and sink his teeth in even harder.

Finally, her hips rose to meet his, urging him to move faster, but Noah refused to do anything but grind against her. He wanted nothing to separate him from the taste of her and the feel of her heart beating for him.

He released her and struck again, sharp wolfie canines sinking into her other breast around her nipple. Noah sucked as much of her tit into his mouth as he could, grinding and rocking against her.

One more bite and she'd come whether she wanted to or not.

Pulling back, he could feel her blood dripping from his teeth, but Noah was too lost in the sweet taste of her and the need to keep claiming her to worry about it.

Harper gasped when he sank his teeth around that spot on her neck that pulsed with the scent and magic of the mate bond. Her blood gushed into his mouth, and she screamed, her entire body clenching around him as she came so hard Noah could barely breathe through the sensation. It took over his entire fucking mind and soul.

She forced him to come for her again, and this time the climax damn near took him out. It required every bit of shifter strength he had not to collapse on top of her as the pleasure mercilessly ripped through him.

It felt so fucking good it hurt and he found himself driving into her over and over, trying to ease some of that sensation as she practically vibrated around him, nails digging into his skin.

Then she did the last thing he'd ever expected from her and sank those tiny little canines into his throat, right over the jugular.

Sharp pain exploded but it was so brief thanks to another fucking climax she forced from him that came right on the heels of the last one.

This time there was no strength left for him to use and Noah whimpered into her throat, shuddering as she sucked on that bite mark *hard.*

She'd claimed him.

His little raven assassin had fucking claimed him, even if it was just for one night. She'd taken it from him like she took everything else, and Noah lost all humanity.

There was nothing left but that feral creature he'd become to survive long enough to protect his twin – to give Liam everything he wasn't capable of having.

His wolf made himself known, snarling as his teeth extended even farther until it felt like his mouth was too full to talk. His deadly claws ripped into the mattress and pillows – feathers exploding as he tore through them to keep from tearing into *her.*

More—he needed so much *more.*

Noah needed to hear her say she was his – he *needed* her to stay even if it meant he was caged and leashed all over again.

Ripping his teeth out of her neck was almost worse than claiming her again. Noah's heart lurched when blood splattered the walls and his pure white sheets.

Had he torn out her fucking throat?

Shit. He'd warned her. He'd warned her he couldn't stop – even now he kept thrusting, sliding a hand between them to ruthlessly rub her clit. Harper orgasmed again, but this time she didn't scream.

She stared at him with wide eyes, so much blood gushing from her throat that he wrapped his hand around it, desperately trying to keep her together while he wrestled with his feral side.

How long had he been lost in his wolf while they lived in those cages, separate and alone? How long had he been forced to stare at the raven in *his* cage and know it was because of that stupid fucking asshole that Liam was in his own cruel cage – alone for the first time in his life?

"Kill me," he begged, heart frantically pounding when her bleeding didn't slow down. "*Kill me* – call Morgan. I can't stop, *please*." The words that fell from his lips were guttural and echoed with both his voice, and his wolf's.

If she died, he'd never forgive himself.

Harper took his face in her hands, and he watched in horror as her eyes dimmed to that pretty honey brown. Seeing it scared him even more.

"Don't stop," she told him, pressing her thumbs to

his canines and drawing even more of her blood. It trickled down her arms and painted her perfect skin. "This is exactly what I wanted."

"You wanted to fucking *die?*" he snarled, squeezing her throat so tight he felt the tendons creak.

"Silly wolf, you could never kill me." Harper pulled his faced down farther and licked her blood from his lips. "You can't kill death, puppy."

Those words didn't reassure him, but Noah slammed into her again and hated himself for relishing in the way she still clenched and pulsed around him, her legs tight around his waist, heels urging him on.

"So pretty," she murmured. "So tasty." Harper *kissed* him, and it shocked him so much he actually stopped.

Completely frozen.

Her lips were gentle as they pressed against his. Then her tongue darted out, licking the seam of his lips. They parted instantly at her soft request and that sweet warmth slid into his mouth and stroked his tongue.

He did nothing. Noah didn't even dare breathe as she explored his mouth, running her tongue over all four of his elongated canines like she was worshipping them and thanking them for the marks all over her body.

What the fuck was happening?

"You did so good," she whispered against his

mouth, sliding her hands into his hair. "Watching you lose control and go truly feral...it was more beautiful than I'd imagined."

There was something really fucking wrong with this girl...

And Noah loved it.

"That's exactly what I wanted to see," she confessed, kissing him again like she actually cared about him. "You said you wanted to taste me, didn't you?"

He was speechless.

"Did I taste as good as you thought?" Harper grinned up at him, waiting for an answer.

This was the time for him to fucking say something —*anything*. Noah should move, he should check her throat, her fucking head...

"There's something wrong with you," he managed to say, voice cracking.

Terror still held his heart hostage and it pounded ruthlessly against his chest. He was too fucking scared to move his hand away from her throat, but she was still conscious so that was something at least.

"Oh, there are a lot of things wrong with me," Harper giggled, pulling him down for another kiss just so she could suck the blood off his lips. "But you like it, don't you?"

He fucking *loved* it.

Noah growled against her mouth, feeling his cock flex inside her.

Why couldn't he ever fucking get soft? What the hell was going on with his body?

"Did you poison me with some kind of sex elixir?" he demanded, searching her eyes for some hint as to what was going on between them. "Why can't I stop fucking you? Why can't I stop coming?"

"I don't know, puppy." She slid her hand down his arm and gently pulled on his wrist.

Noah's fingers flexed around her throat, refusing to release her. He felt his wolf nearly come through his very thin skin and take over as he freaked the fuck out.

What if his hand was the only thing holding her stupid neck together?

"Noah," she whispered, forcing his eyes to lift from her neck to that pretty honey brown again. Her orange hair was a mess and that was almost as distracting as the satisfied smile playing on her lips. "I doubt a claiming mark from my mate would kill me, even one as reckless and vicious as that one."

She'd admitted it.

Out loud.

It was a claiming mark and there was nothing in this world or the next that was going to stop him from seeing it, not even common sense.

Slowly, he removed his hand.

The blood was sticky and pulled at her delicate

skin. Noah winced and stopped, reaching for the water on his nightstand.

"Sorry about this." He didn't wait for her to respond or realize what he was doing – Noah dumped the cup of water over her neck to keep from tearing the freshly healed mark.

Harper cursed at him in a guttural language that made his stomach flip-flop, but he forced himself to ignore it as he used the cleanest part of the ruined bedspread to wipe away some of the blood.

His sharp canines had torn into her, leaving the most vicious claiming mark he'd ever seen. It nearly looked like a forced claim – like the infected ones he'd seen the old Alphas and their favorites give the mates who'd never wanted to be mated or claimed.

It was worse than rape in a way. Once claimed – a wolf could never take it back, not without killing their mate. It would live inside their heart and soul, festering for all of eternity.

So many of them he'd been forced to watch waste away. The stronger ones committed suicide. But the strongest had always tried to kill those wolves. Some of them had even succeeded.

A few of them were still living on their property. They'd shifted into wolves after the death of their mates and hadn't worn their human skin since.

But this brutal claiming mark...it wasn't infected. It was actually partially healed – the marks a pretty pink just like his eyes or the moon...or her salted silver blade still lying on his floor.

"Like what you see, asshole?" Harper demanded through gritted teeth. "Your fucking window is open and it's *freezing*."

His eyes widened in shock, and he stared at her. "You're cold?"

Was it normal for ravens to feel the temperature more like witches, rather than wolves?

Before she could answer the question, he pulled her into his arms and slid off the bed. The attached bathroom should be a little warmer, but he held her close and turned the water on as hot as it would go.

Noah couldn't let go of her.

Harper smelled like blood, sex, desire, and the mate bond. She was *his* and she hadn't denied his claim.

Whether she knew it or not, Noah wasn't going to give this up.

She'd have to fucking kill him if she was going to try to deny it now. There was no going back. He'd gone feral and forced a claim, and...

How had she known it wouldn't kill her? There'd been *so much* blood.

Steam filled the bathroom and her suffocating grip on him loosened just a little. Noah didn't like that, and he held her closer, nails digging into her as his hand spasmed at the thought of her putting any distance between them at all.

This time he was careful not to break her skin. He had no idea how much more of his fucked-up affection she could take without needing a healer or some kind of healing potion.

Burying his face in her neck, right against that mark, helped calm him down enough to ignore the ache in his teeth demanding he put marks all over her fucking body so there was *no way* anyone would ever think she was unclaimed.

He wanted his scent stitched into her bones to warn away anyone with half a nose. If she wanted to torture him and string him along, that was fine. Noah could play these back-and-forth games with her forever because it was better than nothing.

But if she thought he was going to allow her to play those games with *anyone* else, he would dedicate his life to destroying anyone she would spare half a glance for.

He'd kill them all and do it with a grin.

11

HARPER

Hot water ran down her back and she stroked Noah's hair as he stood there with his nose in her neck. He'd been like that for a long time, but she didn't think it was a good idea to move him just yet.

She wanted to keep him.

Noah was such a good puppy, and he would make an even better pet. There was no doubt in her mind that she could collar him and lead him around on a leash if that's what got her to agree to stay with him.

It was tempting.

But she'd left her Collective for freedom. A mate bond didn't automatically take that away from her but being forced to stay in one place would. Harper highly doubted he'd leave his twin.

Why had she let him bite her? Even that first time, she'd wanted it. The ache of his teeth felt so fucking good every single time. Even the last one that had him fucking terrified...

So sweet.

"You owe me answers," she murmured, nibbling his earlobe. "You can do whatever you want to me as long as you answer. If you can't, I'll have to leave."

His entire body tensed, and she saw that black streak through his aura again like lightning. That was the feral part of him she couldn't get enough of, but his wolf wasn't a very good conversationalist.

"I don't want to leave, but I will if you can't uphold your end of the deal." She breathed in his scent, filtering through his vast array of emotions. Then she savored the one underneath that was his true scent.

How did he deal with feeling so many things at once? It seemed exhausting.

"Do you want to keep holding me?" she asked when he didn't move. "Or do you want to wash my hair?"

He tensed again, but she could see the black flicker – warring with a pretty robin's egg blue. Noah desperately wanted to take care of her, but he wanted to keep fucking her too if the still-hard cock branding her stomach was any indication.

This insanity was more than she'd bargained for, but Harper wasn't displeased. If anything, she was impressed. Noah had far more stamina than any shifter she'd ever fucked before. He'd outlasted every feline and canine she'd ever been with, and even most of the bears.

The only one who still had him beat was this snarky raccoon she'd briefly been infatuated with.

Harper had no doubt Noah could beat him too. The night was still relatively young.

"You'd let me wash your hair?" Noah finally asked, rubbing his nose along the bite that took up more than half of her throat.

Harper hoped it scarred.

Maybe she could salt it to make sure it didn't erase the mark of his cruel teeth.

"It's an option." She ran her fingers through his hair again to get it out of his eyes. "Was there something else you'd rather do?"

A deep growl in his chest told her what his wolf wanted.

Harper chuckled and buried her face in his neck, breathing in that feral wolf that reminded her of fur in winter, coated in blood still steaming from his last kill. "Your wolf is delightful."

The way he froze again told her how much Noah hated his wolf.

What a shame.

"Can I see your wolf sometime?" she asked, licking that spot that smelled sweet – like warm caramel and apple cider.

Noah didn't answer, but his entire body started

shaking like he was desperately trying to hold onto his humanity and keep from shifting. No doubt he was big enough to shatter the glass shower.

"Did you know that wolves and ravens used to live in the same packs?" She trailed her nails down the back of his neck to soothe him. "A long time ago, some eyries lived on the ground with wolves. Back then, it was safe for us to nest on the ground instead of the highest eyrie. Wolves protected us and in turn we took care of them. There are paintings of ravens riding on the backs of wolves in my old library."

The shaking got worse, not better. Almost like Noah wanted to shift so she could ride him.

Harper chuckled. She really liked how much he wanted her on top of him.

"Sometimes witches would live with us," she confessed, whispering the words like a secret.

Technically, they were. If the Enclave found out she was whispering their secrets to anyone, they would arrest her and kill Noah, but it wasn't like they'd ever know if he kept his mouth shut.

"Witches still live with ravens, but wolves...so many things changed when witches became neutral. It's a shame so many of them deny their true nature."

Her teeth ached and Harper didn't bother fighting her own instincts. She bit into that caramel apple smell like it was her last dessert. The taste of him and this strange bond exploded on her tongue.

Noah moaned, raking his teeth against her shoulder, like it took everything he had not to bite her —claim her.

That wouldn't do.

She shoved his face against that spot he couldn't resist and held him there by his hair. "Taste me. Leave a mark. Do it, Noah. I want it."

His muscles bulked like he was about to shift, and this time his bite was silent. There was no growl or snarl. Just sharp teeth ripping her skin open.

Sweet Morrigan, it felt so fucking good.

Her head fell back, and she couldn't hold in the groan of pleasure that he coaxed from her.

She wanted to fuck him again.

Harper shoved him away with a snarl, furious with him—with *herself*.

"Answers," she snapped, pointing an accusing finger at him. "Enough with the distractions."

His eyes were half-lidded and glowed like the moon. Noah licked his lips and he looked more wolf than human despite standing on two legs without any fur covering his skin.

The rock-hard cock jutting out kept snagging her attention and Harper licked her own lips, remembering what he tasted like.

"Ask me," he growled, taking a step toward her. "Hurry."

He felt this insanity too.

Maybe it wasn't a purposeful distraction, but something neither of them could resist.

"Why did you challenge an Alpha?" she gritted out, taking a step back.

The water nearly drowned her, but she glared at him, ignoring it even though it made the smell of blood stronger.

"Because I can," he snarled, gripping her arm and yanking her forward.

"*Why?*" she hissed. "The real reason."

Those silver eyes glowed so brightly it actually hurt her eyes. "Because, this way, it only costs one life. Mine is the least valuable. I do not have a mate – not one who wants me anyway."

Harper had the most interesting physical reaction to that. She actually heaved like she was going to throw up and it surprised her so much, she stared at Noah in shock.

What the fuck was that?

"What happens if you win?" she asked, pulling out of his hold to rest a trembling hand on her stomach. Such a weird reaction. "Will you become their Alpha?"

Noah barked out a laugh that was anything but humorous. "As if anyone would listen to me."

She frowned. "Then what happens?"

He sighed then and eyed the contents of the shower before slicking his hair back. "Defeating an

Alpha doesn't automatically make the victor the Alpha of that pack. They have a choice, and so does the pack."

Harper didn't know enough about the intricacies of wolf hierarchy to understand how that would work, and she'd never heard of a submissive immune to an Alpha's power before.

Maybe it was because he was a twin? Shifter twins were always special somehow, even among ravens. Harper frowned again and wondered if triplets existed, and if they did...what would they be capable of?

"The victor can choose to 'retire' and give the pack over to someone worthy and capable of leading it," Noah explained.

Every movement was stiff as he bent down and reached for the shampoo.

"Now, peaceful transitions are more common than violent ones, but not for my pack. Every Alpha was challenged constantly, and the fights were always to the death – death isn't required, but if that wolf loses, they can't stay within the pack and sometimes...they'd rather die than admit defeat."

He crooked his finger at her and watched with those slitted eyes as she considered whether she wanted to let him wash her hair now.

"Come here, Harper," Noah growled, those claws at the tips of his fingers elongating ever so slightly.

Such a bossy brat for a submissive.

"Maybe I don't want to," she sniffed, crossing her arms over her chest.

"Lies." Noah was fast when he wanted to be.

Suddenly, he was right in front of her, thumb caressing the fresh bite mark on her neck. It was sore but she closed her eyes at the sensation. That he liked it so much made her feel...satisfied.

It wasn't quite an emotion, but it felt like eating a delicious meal and then being totally and completely sated afterward.

Fascinating that he could make her feel anything at all, even like this.

"Tell me you want it," he murmured, that echo of his wolf vibrating along her skin like a thousand kisses. "Then I'll keep talking."

"Fine." Harper turned around, watching the blood sluice down her body and swirl down the drain. "Now finish explaining it to me."

So she could fuck him again, right there in the shower. This time she could use the water to nearly drown him, edging him instead of overstimulating him. Maybe then he would finally cry for her.

"You didn't say it," he whispered into her ear, making her shiver. "Use your words, Harper. I want to *hear* it."

Those claws tickled when he pressed a hand to her belly, forcing her back against him. Instantly, the nausea disappeared.

His ridiculous, rock-hard cock nestled between the cheeks of her ass, taunting her with its heat. Every time it flexed, she clenched her jaw, reminding herself she wanted answers first.

"I'll do you one better."

Pressing back against him, she trailed the tips of her nails over his thighs and wriggled until his cock flexed so hard Noah's sharp inhale nearly stole the air from the fucking room.

"Noah, sweet wolf, would you please wash my hair?" she asked, digging her nails into his thighs just like he'd done to her. The scent of his blood was intoxicating. She wanted to bathe in it instead of the water. "I want you to wash my hair, puppy."

His shuddering breath told her she had the upper hand yet again. Harper leaned her head back against his pecs and smiled when he silently started washing her hair.

It was adorable how his hands shook.

"If the pack doesn't like the victor, they can choose to challenge them," Noah continued quietly, his fingers gently working the shampoo into her hair. "That only happens if the victor chooses to lead the pack, but one dominant wolf doesn't always have the skill to defeat another dominant wolf. True alphas are rare, and the strength of their alpha command strengthens or weakens depending on their pack."

Well, that was something she hadn't known.

Harper wondered if the Cascade Alpha had a good connection to his pack.

"Sometimes, you can petition the Council to step in if an Alpha is abusing their power, but it's easier to hire a hunter or an assassin." Noah's hand slid back to her belly, directing them both so he could wash the soap from her hair. "None of us could afford an assassin, and the Council is run by witches for the most part. They don't care about shifters. Neither do vampires. That leaves hunters, and even they're expensive."

Was she feeling...something? Harper didn't understand the heavy feeling in her chest. There was no way she cared about his past, and yet, the idea of him locked in a cage still lingered uncomfortably in the back of her mind.

Maybe Valentina could take that memory from her later.

"It's hard to make friends with people outside the pack, and even more difficult when the people you care about are little more than slaves to an Alpha who wants to abuse them."

Noah's voice was strained, his wolf retreating. Harper recognized that tone though – the desperate yearning for freedom.

"I stayed for my twin. Then for Shane and Alexander." The sickly-sweet scent of melancholy filled her nose and Harper was not fond of it. "I tried to hire a hunter at one point, but they were killed unfortunately. That was the last time I tried anything. More innocent lives weighing on my soul wasn't something I could handle."

"That's the difference between you and me, puppy." Harper turned around and gripped his cock so hard Noah hissed at her, but otherwise he didn't move. "I kill anyone and everyone who stands between me and what I want, whether they're innocent or not."

Surprisingly, Noah smiled down at her. "Where have you been all my life?"

And he thought there was something wrong with *her?*

"I want to fuck you in here," she told him, pulling him closer by his dick.

Then she gripped his shoulder where her bite mark lingered and shoved him down, forcing him to his knees. Harper got lost in the way he looked up at her, ready and waiting for whatever she decided to do next.

Settling one leg over his shoulder, she ran her fingertips over his lips, admiring their fullness and just how swollen they looked after all the abuse. A gentle push with her leg was all it took, and he leaned into her, hands reverently sliding up her calves.

"Before I fuck you until you cry, you're going to suck me until I scream," she murmured, entranced by his instant obedience. "Does that sound like something you want?"

Noah nodded. Then he licked her long and slow, flicking her clit at the top, and he never once looked away from her face. His hands gripped her thighs and pulled her closer until she was sure he was going to suffocate.

Gripping his hair, she held him there, closing her eyes as she indulged in the pleasure that washed away all the uncomfortable sensations.

Her orgasm hovered close, making her legs shake as he sucked and licked, sliding two, thick fingers inside her to ease some of the ache.

How did he always get her to orgasm so quickly? It fucked with her thoughts and made her lose time when he did this.

Noah had earned her kiss and her decision, proving he was as perfect as she'd thought.

"Don't worry, puppy," she murmured, grinding against him. "You're too good at this to kill."

Just like that, he growled against her clit, his wolf vibrating in his chest – through her, and shattering her to pieces in his arms.

12

HARPER

Dawn caressed her skin and Harper blinked against the rosy light, realizing she was still in bed with the wolf.

She didn't remember falling asleep.

Harper ignored the sudden pounding of her heart as she sifted through the scents in the room.

Blood touched everything. The sheets were still ripped and ruined. Noah hadn't changed them or the blanket. They were lying in a bed full of cum and blood.

And yet, she'd never been more comfortable.

She was warm, and the arm around her middle felt right. It wasn't too heavy or too hot. Fingertips brushed against her belly instead of claws and Harper swallowed down her disappointed sigh.

Why she liked him on the edge of feral, she didn't

know. Noah was harder to control when his wolf decided to get involved, but he fucked her like he wanted to kill her when he lost all sense of humanity.

That's what she liked about him, she supposed.

Noah wasn't just a human who sometimes turned into a wolf. He was a wolf in sheep's clothing – submissive and willing to please, but he was vicious and cruel about it, and it made her fucking mouth water every time she wondered how he was going to punish her with his compliance next time.

This submissive puppy had fucked her into oblivion even after she'd given him enough orgasms to rattle his brain. Too bad he hadn't let her edge him, but the way he'd eaten her pussy made up for it.

She could always edge him next time.

Now he slept harder than the dead, and she wondered if he would wake up when she moved.

For once, Harper didn't want to wake up someone she'd had sex with because she wanted to avoid their attempts to see her again, but because Noah needed the rest.

She'd done worse to him than she usually did to the people she interrogated, and he'd loved every second of it.

Well, maybe not the part where he'd thought he'd killed her.

Still...

Her fingers touched the sore spot on her neck that

lingered. Why she wanted it to scar was something Harper wasn't ready to think about.

It was past dawn. She should go.

Instead, she lay there, enjoying the cool breeze from the window thanks to the heater Noah was when he slept. If she didn't know better, she'd think he had a fever.

Taking inventory of those in the house, Harper listened and counted each heartbeat she recognized. Thanks to the magic stitched into her spine, their pitiful wards to soundproof each bedroom didn't work on her.

Even the new wards around the house weren't quite strong enough to cancel out her magic, but it did glitch and Harper looked up, sensing the witch on the roof.

Morgan.

She didn't have the time to wonder why she'd *slept* with Noah after the sex. Harper didn't want to look at it too closely, and she certainly didn't want him to wake up and see she was still there.

Stupid wolf might think he'd won something.

Every skill she'd ever learned as an assassin kept her from waking him up as she slid out of the bed. There was no sound to disturb him either as she picked up her charms from the nightstand.

One silent snap of her fingers and she was fully dressed and armed.

Pulling the necklace over her head, she grabbed her knife off the floor and slipped into the shadow realm, jumping up onto the windowsill in one smooth motion. Then she dropped into a crouch.

Harper refused to look back at him, no matter how badly she wanted to.

She pushed off the window and threw her body as far from the building as she could. Harper shifted mid-air, flapping her wings hard as she flew through the shadow realm, higher and higher.

That witch was no doubt waiting for her.

Harper would never get used to Seers. It didn't matter that every eyrie had one, they were all fucking creepy, but she couldn't say their skills didn't balance out the lack of privacy.

She circled far above that roof, eyeing the witch who was lying on one of the lounge chairs. Those light brown eyes seemed to see right through the shadow realm and all her magic to exactly where Harper was.

It may have been an optical illusion, but raven eyesight was better than all the other shifters except owls, and that unwavering gaze followed her in a circle over and over without ever once blinking.

Finding out what kind of Seer this witch was would be vital to her and Valentina's plans. If she couldn't charm her, they may as well kiss any chance of making this work in their favor good-bye.

Harper arrowed down, shooting for the roof at a breakneck speed.

If she had any doubts the witch could see her before, she didn't now, not when that spooky gaze unerringly followed her path.

Shifting just before hitting the ground, her knees bent at precisely the right time to cushion her descent.

Harper straightened and stared down at the witch lounging before her, one arm back behind her head to act as a pillow with a flirty smile playing on her lips.

Even though Harper was still in the shadow realm.

This one had to be a dark witch then. If she could see through the veil, then she was either a shadow witch or...a night witch? Necromancers could sometimes figure out the veil, but the shadows weren't natural for them.

Only one other dark witch could use the shadow realm like a raven, but they were extinct now.

On an exhale, she stepped through the glittering shroud that separated their world from the shadow realm, and slowly lifted her charms over her head. Harper could have left them on, but this would help her start their conversation on the right foot.

"I don't think I've ever seen anyone who can shift like you do," Morgan admitted, eyes dropping to the charms. "You waited until the very last second, and yet your hair didn't even get ruffled by the wind."

It sounded like a compliment, but Harper didn't think it was.

"I'm a little peeved I spent so much money on these charms, and yet, you can still see me." She tossed the necklace to Morgan, and the witch caught it like a pro.

She wasn't as fast as a shifter, but faster than an average witch. Morgan hadn't blinked either, so she could See clearly even without having to meditate or activate some kind of vision.

Her aura was a strange shade of pink too – like... the darkest pink that still managed to edge into that obnoxiously vibrant Barbie color. She tilted her head and tried to figure out what it reminded her of.

There was a witch with hair that color actually, but the taste of Morgan's magic didn't have the essence of the shadow realm, so she wasn't a shadow witch, and the magic didn't taste like death, so not a necromancer either.

"There are so very few of you left," Harper said, looking away from the witch. "What is a powerful night witch doing meddling in shifter affairs?"

Her eyes skimmed the roof and then paused on the herbs Noah had hung up to dry, and she wondered if he'd ever be open to helping her maintain her weapons.

Morgan giggled.

The sound made Harper want to scrape the sensation off her skin with her salted blade. She couldn't help the grimace when whatever emotion *that* was felt like chewing on tin foil.

"I'm curious, how did you know?" Morgan inspected the charms on the necklace, still reclining like she didn't have a care in the world despite having a raven assassin looming over her.

"There's a night witch on the East Coast," Harper admitted. "She was the one who made those charms."

"Faye O'Riley?" Morgan asked, tossing them back to Harper.

She caught them effortlessly and then tucked them into her back pocket. "The one and only."

"I wouldn't say your money was wasted," Morgan said, looking Harper up and down. Her thumb spun one of the rings on her index finger over and over. "There are only a dozen witches on this continent who are stronger than Faye, if we don't count the other nasties."

Right, and those assholes were exactly why she'd stayed out of the free cities despite the lack of allegiance she would owe.

Harper inspected the witch. Morgan looked totally relaxed in the presence of a raven. Her aura was calm and stable too, despite the dark color. Nothing about her posture or aura fooled Harper though. The magic she possessed could destroy her without even really trying...but only if the witch was faster than a raven.

"You must have known we were here before Noah

did. Why didn't you say anything? I know you were watching us yesterday." Harper crossed her arms over her chest but didn't blink or look away from the witch.

Morgan's slight smile stretched into a grin. It was slow, like watching the sun rise in the morning.

It was unsettling.

"I didn't want to," the witch stated, twirling that damn ring around and around.

Harper held the witch's gaze for a long time, neither of them blinking. It wasn't quite a dominance game like the wolves played, but it was *something*.

Morgan's eyes started to glow pink then, reminding Harper just how powerful she was. Only the strongest witches' magic affected their eyes like a shifter's, as if it was just too much for their body to contain.

Finally, the witch blinked slowly, like she might just fall asleep if she didn't hurry up and open her eyes. "Would you like me to look into your future, Harper of Storm Ridge?"

13

HARPER

The blood in her veins chilled.

Such a simple question shouldn't garner that kind of reaction, but Harper didn't like the way it felt as though the universe was listening, curious what her answer would be.

Morgan waited patiently, still spinning her ring.

Wasn't she supposed to be the one getting the intel? Harper mentally shook herself. Just because this witch was a spooky bitch, she wasn't going to be distracted even if the possibility of knowing whether she'd succeed in her endeavors or not was so tempting and shiny she'd nearly agreed.

"No, thank you."

Harper didn't look away even when that pink aura shifted ever so slightly through the darkest pinks. Purple began to cloud it, but not in a way that indicated anything was wrong. Rather, it looked like a drop of purple ink, swirling in water like pretty smoke clouds.

It didn't alter the color of the pink base, but it told Harper...something. This witch was hard to read, and that made her even more curious.

"Have you been trained by ravens?" she asked, unable to help herself.

Morgan's smile widened, and this one put Harper at ease despite how sharp it was. "You're extremely perceptive, even for a raven."

It was impossible not to preen.

"Corbin and Emily are still better than you."

"But not more perceptive," Harper snapped, planting her hands on her hips. "You don't have to be a bitch, you know. I have no intention of killing you."

"But you still haven't decided which side to pick," Morgan pointed out. She sat up and wrapped her arms around her legs, somehow looking like a child despite her age. "I still See two variations of a future that rest in your pretty little claws. It's making me sick having to watch them both. Just decide already."

"Why do you even care?"

Tucking a stray piece of hair behind her ear, Morgan adjusted the oversized gray sweater she had on. It almost looked like a dress, and she wore it with a pair of black leather pants.

"If the Blue Mountain Pack falls to the Cascade Range Pack, the Pacific Northwest will not be strong enough to defend against what's to come. We need strong packs and prides ready to defend our territories – shifters who won't shy away from working with witches."

A chill went down her spine and Harper *really* didn't like how those words sounded like prophecy.

"Did you know there is a fox den nearby?" the witch asked, watching Harper closely. "Plus, two raven eyries and a pack of coyotes that conveniently keep to themselves. Then there is the traveling circus here in Portland that is technically a pride, but it's also an active Sanctuary. They don't just have lions, but wolves, humans, and witches. I hear they even have a vampire. The Cirque de Nuit has a very strong alliance with the Blue Mountain Pack now, thanks to Lily and Alexander being mates."

What the fuck was the point of this? Anyone with half a brain knew all that. Harper didn't really care about all the paranormal drama, not unless someone paid for her to care about it.

"The point is, there are plenty of shifters and witches who already work well together," Morgan pointed out as she glanced at the door that led into the townhouse. "We make up for each other's weaknesses, and our world needs more of that. It's why I've adopted the Klamath Mountain Pride as my personal project.

Well, I did grow up in it, so I suppose it's only natural I chose them first."

Harper didn't know what to say to that. It was rare for a witch to grow up with shifters unless they were ravens.

The traveling circus Sanctuary was the only other group of shifters she knew of who took in orphaned witches, but they tended to avoid the dark ones because of their Sanctuary status.

Unlike ravens.

Harper considered all the potential reasons a witch who possessed Sight so strong she'd willingly crossed the invisible line separating witches and shifters – a line that had existed for hundreds of years.

"You're trying to change shifters' opinions of witches?" Harper asked, dying to know what futures she'd seen and why she wanted to avoid them so badly.

Morgan nodded.

"But not witches' opinions of shifters?" Harper rolled her eyes. "Typical clan witch behavior."

Those pretty brown eyes narrowed, and Morgan swung her legs around, planting her feet on the ground with enough intention it felt like the universe shook a little.

"First of all, I'm not the witch who will change the opinion of other witches. She will manage far better than I with her royal blood. And second of all, I am not a recognized clan witch, or I wouldn't have had to grow up in a pride, now would I?" Morgan slowly stood, and Harper realized then that the witch was the same exact height as her, not taller. "Witches don't like me or my Sight. I barely got accepted into the Midnight Coven after months of testing. So, why would I give them the benefit of my help for free?"

That actually made more sense.

Harper grinned. "You should charge them more."

"I have other plans for the witches," Morgan murmured, taking a step forward and somehow it felt like the temperature dropped the closer she got. "But shifters? They need my help if we're going to survive what's coming."

She bit on her tongue hard enough to taste blood instead of giving Morgan the satisfaction of asking what it was they had to survive.

"There are still children of Death," Morgan murmured, closing the distance between them. She smelled like stars and...darkness. "Ravens aren't the only ones despite how many black feathers have been in so many of my visions."

Harper took a step back and she bared her teeth at the witch, irritated that the power dynamics had shifted somehow. The sudden drop in temperature was making her shiver despite all her training.

"There are a few banshees left, some necromancers, and from what I can tell, there are night witches other than just Faye and me. Technically...any of the witches who derive from Hecate are also children of Death even if they don't possess the necromancy skills."

Banshees were supposed to be extinct, but ravens had been hiding them away in their eyries for generations. It was the only way to protect them when so many *things* hunted them down like animals.

Did that mean there could be others hidden away that they thought were lost?

"Do you believe in the Morrigan?" the witch asked, tilting her head. "She created raven shifters and so you call her the raven queen, don't you?"

That question made Harper freeze, and it almost felt like blasphemy to hear her goddess's name on a witch's lips outside of an eyrie. Her blade made of silver was suddenly in her hand and ready as she waited for Morgan to get to the fucking point.

"Clearly you know what I'm talking about, which means you also know she is the goddess of death and war and magic."

Harper would have said something except there wasn't that sickly-sweet taste of melancholy and despair. Instead, it tasted like steel and...belladonna – a witch who knew how to use poisons and wasn't afraid of the consequences would do whatever was necessary to see her vision become reality.

"Do you know of the Morrigan's children?" Morgan asked.

"We do," Harper admitted, not seeing the harm in confirming what this dark witch already knew.

"Ravens aren't her only children." Morgan took another step forward, spinning the ring on her finger as she stared at Harper with that creepy, unblinking gaze. "Blood witches, banshees, and even some necromancers are also her children."

"And all the blood witches are dead," Harper hissed, her grip on the silver knife tightening. "Every raven knows this. What's the point of reminding me how badly we failed at protecting them? What's the fucking point of *any* of this?"

"What if I told you that they're not all dead?"

She froze, wanting to deny it, but this was a night witch.

"What if I *also* told you that despite what it might look like, Noah is far more open to freedom than you'd think?"

Harper narrowed her eyes. "Why should I believe anything you say?"

Quick as lightning, Morgan *moved*, her long ponytail swinging forward as she wrapped her fingers around Harper's jaw. Sharp black nails dug into her cheeks as Morgan gripped her face hard enough it actually hurt.

When had the bitch even moved?

Something in Morgan's eyes again flared to life, shifting the light brown to a strange glowy pink. "Want me to prove it to you?" she asked, pulling Harper closer.

She glared at the witch, wondering how much she could See, and how much of it was just digging through surface thoughts. Maybe she read auras too, it was hard to tell with the dark ones.

Did she want to get dragged through visions until she lost her sanity? No, that wasn't something she was interested in doing again no matter how much the mystery begged for her to unravel it.

"If you can do it without rifling through my head, sure." Harper watched the witch and her aura closely, ready to cut her hand from her arm if she had to.

The touch on her face was so cold it burned.

"You are a curious one, aren't you, little raven?" Morgan was so close her freezing cold breath washed over Harper's skin like death. "It's what drives you, even without your emotions on. And it's why you can't stop coming back to Noah. He's not defective, but special, and you can see it."

The idea of staying with wolves and living a boring life was repulsive.

Nothing could change the reality of Noah's situation. He lived on land that they called a homestead with other wolves in a place where almost nothing ever happened.

Even if she still worked as an assassin, the days in between jobs would be worse than living in the eyrie with the insufferable shadow of Emily and Corbin hanging over her.

Harper hadn't ever wanted to be 'the best,' but she'd excelled, and it still hadn't satisfied that restless part of her that was never satisfied no matter if she had her emotions on or not.

What would she even *do* every day? Fucking him all day and night wouldn't keep her entertained forever.

Noah would want to stay with his brother and watching those wolves for only a week had made her want to rip her hair out just to alleviate the boredom.

"Are you sure he wants to stay?" Morgan asked, searching Harper's eyes. "Maybe he's ready to finally leave the place that gives him nightmares whether his twin wants to or not."

"I don't care about this pack, Morgan. I will choose the right path for *me*, and no one else."

"I've kept an eye on him ever since I saw the future no one else can see," the night witch murmured, angling Harper's face like she could somehow see beneath the skin. "There are still too many possibilities, but if you reject him, he'll self-destruct and that wolf, and his twin, currently hold this pack together. If they die...the future I've seen without them isn't one I would wish on my worst enemy."

"Why would I want a mate?" she asked the witch, raising one eyebrow. Knocking the hand off her face was long overdue. Harper considered this witch and wondered how her choosing Noah worked in her benefit. "Why do *you* want me to have one? How does it benefit this pack? Aren't they you're little pet project?"

"Among others," Morgan agreed. "Do you want me to give you my honest answer, or the one that'll make you feel better?"

Curiosity gripped Harper by the throat and shook her, demanding she know the truth.

"You may not want a mate," Morgan conceded, smiling slightly. "But you don't want anyone else to have him either."

Harper glared and reconsidered her plan to let this witch live.

Before she could say or do *anything*, Morgan pulled her into the shadow realm and pressed a finger to her lips, grinning like an idiot.

The wolves are coming, Morgan whispered into her mind. *This isn't how they should find you.*

Two males she didn't recognize came up on the roof with cups of coffee, and Harper decided it was time to leave.

Call your partner.

The sensation of someone else's thoughts in her head made Harper want to scream.

Then meet me at the café on the corner when you decide what to do.

Morgan released her and it was suddenly impossible to see the witch, like her entire being became the veil.

There was no time to unravel *that* particular mystery no matter how shiny.

At least, not right now.

Harper ran toward the ledge of the roof and leapt off, throwing her body into the sky. She let gravity take hold of her for a brief moment, knowing if she didn't shift, she'd plummet to her death.

Before it was too late, she shifted, coasting through the veil as she considered everything that had happened in the last twenty-four hours.

It was time to call Valentina.

Right after she went and spied on this wolf Alpha who would willingly let Noah take his place.

14

NOAH

"Noah?"

He looked up and realized Olivia had probably said his name a few times now if the worried frown on her face was any indication.

"Are you okay?" she asked. Olivia pressed against his shoulder, snuggling against him on the couch in the living room.

Back at the homestead in La Grande thanks to an emergency pack meeting.

Noah bit back a sigh and wrapped his arm around Olivia's shoulders so she didn't feel alone with all the mated pairs filling up a living room that suddenly felt too small.

When Kai had originally built this house, Noah had thought it had been too much – too grossly overdone. No one needed a mansion in the woods even if it was posing as a cabin.

They did all used to live in this house though, and then the mated pairs started moving out into the individual houses their thoughtful Alpha had built for them, anticipating the growth of their pack.

When Kai had taken over, Noah hadn't really believed their pack would ever reach this stage.

Now it was just him, Olivia, Liam, and Zoe in the main house with Kai and Amelia. The others had all moved to their own houses on the property and settled in.

Zoe had chosen to stay in the main house for him and Liam. Sometimes he wondered how someone so prickly could care so much, but then again, he knew she cared, Zoe just showed it differently.

Unlike Harper.

Surprisingly, the raven hadn't taken any of his memories this time. Every moment until he'd fallen asleep with her was still there, and he hadn't woken up with a blinding migraine.

Just an empty, ruined bed.

Harper hadn't erased her blood or his either. Noah hadn't known what to do with the whole thing, so he'd just left it, and locked the door when Liam told him they had to go back to La Grande.

His confession about alphas had apparently caused an uproar.

Kai still refused to let him do this, and Noah refused to let his Alpha die for their pack.

It was unlikely Kai could lose, but Noah wasn't going to risk it, not again. If Kai lost, everything would go back to the way it was, and he would rather die than watch that happen again.

This time he was an adult – *this* time, he would hunt down and kill every wolf in Cascade just like he had Matteo earlier that day.

A knock on the door made his shoulders tense, but Noah could smell the felines. Running into them during his little hunt had been...something.

Harper was gone and Noah didn't think he'd ever see her again. What incentive did she have to come find him if she wasn't going to kill him? He almost wished she hadn't promised him that.

"No one rush to answer the door," Amelia muttered, jogging down the stairs toward the front door.

"They're here for you, not us," Liam teased, bumping Noah with his elbow. "Alpha business and all that."

Noah slid his gaze over to Liam and studied his twin closely.

His mate had her hand settled possessively on Liam's thigh, and her sharp eyes took in everything. Zoe ignored the original pack members and their mates for the most part and kept her attention on Chris and the newly bitten wolves.

That one had no allegiance to Kai, and sometimes Noah wondered what that would look like when push came to shove.

Amelia opened the door and stepped aside for the lion Alpha, his Second, and his Third. Between the three of them was Kitty, their mate. Olivia perked up beside him and twisted so she could watch them together.

"I'll never get over that," she murmured.

Noah didn't bother to look. He didn't need to see them to know what she was talking about. His stomach was in knots already, for so many reasons.

Was Calvin going to fucking tell on him?

He couldn't decide if he was more annoyed at the lions, or Harper. It was her fucking fault he'd gone off the deep end and hunted a human during the day.

Not that Matteo had deserved to live, but still.

The last thing he needed today was another lecture from the lion Alpha which would only get Kai on his case too, and they currently weren't speaking to each other.

Kai was *not* pleased with him.

Noah knew it wasn't because he'd hidden the truth from him, but because he refused to back down on this, and then Kai had gotten to see firsthand how the Alpha command couldn't force him to do shit if he didn't want to.

There was still one little secret he was keeping, and Noah glanced at his twin again. They'd never told anyone about it, and that secret had saved their lives more times than they could count.

People talking filtered through his thoughts, but he was spacing out again. Noah couldn't stop thinking about his pretty little raven and the way she tasted.

The thick, cloying taste of her blood lingered on his tongue, and he kept imagining he could smell her sweet mango mixed in with the scent of feathers and the night sky. It was actually nice that he couldn't smell her emotions on top of everything else.

But why had she chosen to spare his life? Did that mean she'd spare the others? Or was it just him?

Noah was still furious he hadn't woken up when she'd slipped out of the bed.

She'd finally worn him out, even though it hadn't felt like it would ever happen at the time.

And then he'd woken up to find his arms empty.

It was the first time in his life he'd actually felt cold.

There was nothing to track her with outside his room and the roof. Harper was gone, and she hadn't left a way to contact her.

Noah figured she could easily find him if she wanted to, but...*did* she want to? Had he left enough of an impression to make her want to seek him out for more comfort, even if it was just physical?

As long as she came back, he didn't care, but Noah was slowly losing his mind wondering over and over again if she would. His thoughts were spiraling, and nothing could hold his attention.

Liam had tried to say something to him a few times now, but every time he was about to open his mouth, someone interrupted them. It almost felt like fate, and Noah wondered if maybe there was something else at work.

Why else would Morgan be involved?

"Good to see you, Noah," Damien said quietly from behind him, placing a hand on his shoulder and squeezing. "We heard some interesting news."

He rolled his eyes.

Of course they had.

An excited squeal nearly pierced his eardrums as Lily came running from the front yard. She jumped and wrapped her arms around Calvin, hugging the grumpy Alpha tight.

Lily smelled like earth and the feral wolves in the forest. She'd probably been in the new greenhouse with her brother.

Cole walked in a second later, his hands in his pockets, and a huge grin on his face as he watched his sister maul the Alpha. Kitty was giggling, and even Amelia was smiling.

It made him want to shift and take off into the forest to join the feral wolves. Noah would run the perimeter with them just like he did every time he patrolled, and it wouldn't take his wolf long to silence all his human thoughts.

Sometimes the only reason he shifted back into his human form was because Liam wanted him to. Otherwise, Noah could do all the human shit as a wolf.

Well, watching TV was weird considering how fucked up the colors looked when he was in his wolf form.

"Noah?" Damien hadn't been distracted by the witch, and Noah winced.

"I'm sure we'll get to talk about it soon," Noah murmured, eyeing Liam to see if he'd noticed.

Yup, that glare was there and the only thing keeping him from wrestling Noah to the ground was Zoe's sharp nails digging into his thigh.

Noah loved the shit out of her.

He wondered if Harper would like her.

Closing his eyes, he wished for a split second that she'd stolen his memories again. This was fucking torture.

"I appreciate all your help, Calvin," Kai was saying, directing the other Alpha to one of the many chairs.

The house was built for these kinds of gatherings, but all the people and smells were starting to make

Noah nauseous. Maybe he should just wait for them all to go to bed and then take off.

He'd handle the Cascade Alpha on his own if he had to.

But the feral wolves would probably tell on him if the new wards didn't.

It was more work than he'd prefer to keep his facial expression neutral when all he wanted to do was glare at nothing and curse that fucking witch for sticking her nose in his business.

Couldn't she go bother literally *anyone* else?

Maybe she could find Harper.

Noah slowly let out a breath and forced himself to watch the lions and the witches get comfortable among their pack of wolves. The humans still looked anxious and out of place, and most of them weren't mated so they had to be feeling adrift after getting ripped from their normie lives.

Alexander was in charge of them, and he was far more patient and understanding than Noah could ever be. The big, soft wolf was currently in the city though, holding down the fort with those other two newly bitten.

Hopefully, he didn't go in Noah's room. That was a conversation he wasn't ever going to be ready to have.

With anyone.

"So, you're going to challenge Cascade?" Calvin asked, eyes briefly flicking to Noah.

"I am," Kai agreed, pulling Amelia into his lap.

Amelia didn't argue with him, but her eyes glowed silver. They'd been mated for a few months now, and she'd had her first shift. Amelia was a natural alpha, but she wasn't as dominant as Kai.

She wasn't happy about this. At all.

Noah wondered if they'd been planning for pups before all this happened. This pack could do with some babies once everything was safe again. He missed having more than one generation, and if Jacob's parents moved back, maybe Kai could bring his.

That would be nice.

"Actually, *I* am going to challenge Cascade," Noah corrected, ignoring the way Olivia stiffened beside him. "As I'm sure everyone already knows, and clearly disagrees with. I'm the only one without a mate."

"And I keep telling you that's not true," Olivia snapped, eyes flashing silver. "If anyone other than Kai is going to challenge that asshole, it should be me."

Lily looked like she was going to say something, but Calvin saved his ass whether he knew it or not.

Those glowing gold eyes swung to Noah with feline interest. "Supposedly you can defy an Alpha's command and power even though you're a submissive? I've never heard of this."

"It's a twin thing," Liam said carefully, "Shifter twins can be born with weird gifts. I'm surprised you didn't know that considering how old and well established your pride is."

Zoe was definitely rubbing off on him, and Noah smirked, pleased with this new sass his brother had. Usually, he left the arguing up to Noah.

Sliding his gaze to the left, he caught Zoe's eye and she smirked right back at him.

She was perfect.

"Regardless," Kai cut in, that deep rumble in his chest indicating how bothered he was by all this. "I'm not letting someone I'm supposed to protect take my place in a dangerous fight. If you lost, I'd never forgive myself."

Kai's alpha instincts were riding him hard, and Noah knew there was no way he was going to win this argument even if he proved that he wasn't lying yet again. Calvin wouldn't let him do it either and he wasn't even Noah's Alpha.

Dominant shifters were such a fucking pain in the ass sometimes.

"Look, this wouldn't even be a problem if we'd taken care of Cascade when they'd attacked Jacob," Noah pointed out, ignoring the collective inhale from every fucking wolf in that room. "Unless there is a one hundred percent chance you're going to win the challenge, I can't let you die, Alpha. I refuse to do this all over again."

Shane looked like he was about to beat his ass, but Kai held up a hand, holding Noah's gaze.

The urge to look down still tugged at him, but he didn't have to if he didn't want to. Noah looked down at Kai's chin out of respect, acknowledging that he'd done well providing for this pack.

But he had hesitated when it came to protecting them. As a wolf who hadn't been at war his whole life, Noah could forgive that, but he wasn't going to let this shit fall apart.

Not again.

"Then I'll make sure there is a one hundred percent chance I will win," Kai told him, his voice strong and sure with the kind of promise only a dominant could give.

Noah believed him, but he still wasn't willing to risk it, not when his mate looked like she'd do *anything* to keep Kai alive.

Still, he bit his tongue instead of arguing.

There was another way, he just had to find it.

Olivia said something but he didn't hear it because all his senses shifted to the soft knock at the door.

Why hadn't he scented something coming this fucking close to the door?

Shane beat him there, but it was Kai who opened the door, wicked fast just like most Alphas.

"Hello," Morgan said, smiling wide as she took the three of them in.

That wasn't who had his heart pounding so hard he thought it might just give out. No, it was the woman with short, curly orange hair standing next to Morgan like they'd known each other forever.

"I brought a friend," Morgan murmured, eyes shifting from Kai to Noah. "I hope you don't mind."

Holy shit, Harper was at his fucking house.

Noah almost threw up right then and there, but he managed to swallow down the bile as he stared at his raven assassin.

She wouldn't even look at him.

A slow, feral grin spread across his face, and Noah felt his teeth ache as the canines elongated.

Harper was going to regret showing up here after abandoning him, and he couldn't *wait* to remind her you can't just abandon a puppy and get away with it.

15

NOAH

His eyes were locked onto Harper's neck, but she was wearing some black long-sleeved shirt that went all the way up to her chin.

Were his marks still there? Had they healed?

"This is Harper," Morgan said, but she sounded far away when all he could focus on was the lack of scent and sound around them both. "She's a raven and has agreed to do me a favor."

The memory of her blood on his tongue and the feel of being inside her made Noah take a step forward, and he was shocked when something held him back.

"Noah," Shane warned, holding on to his shoulder so tightly it made the bones creak. "I know she's a raven, but she's Morgan's friend."

That's when he realized he was growling deep in his chest.

Harper finally looked at him, but her face was a mask of nothing and that only made his growl turn into a snarl as his lip curled in disgust.

Why was she hiding from him? What the fuck was she even *doing* here? This had to be more punishment...or something. Noah didn't understand what the fuck was going on, and neither did anyone else.

Except for Morgan.

"She agreed to help train Kai, and this pack," Morgan said, still looking at Noah with this smile on her face that made him snarl at *her*.

"*Noah.*" Kai's sharp voice and Shane shaking him still couldn't cut through the haze of hatred and need.

She'd *left* him.

Noah knocked his Alpha and the Second off of him and closed the distance between him and Harper. He stared down at her, feeling the need to mark her all over again.

He couldn't see it – couldn't smell it.

The Alpha was shocked all over again that Noah could just ignore him like that, and it gave him the time he needed to get close enough to touch her. But somehow, he managed to keep his hands to himself.

And Harper...she didn't move despite the way he'd practically pounced on her. No, she just looked up at him with her pretty honey-brown eyes and smiled. "Hello wolfie."

Oh, god, he wanted—he *needed* her to touch him. Something—*anything* that told him she remembered the night before and had wanted it just as badly as he had.

"Can I help you?" Harper asked, tilting her head to the side.

Noah snickered, hating her for playing this stupid game, but he couldn't help but laugh considering how clueless everyone else was.

Noah tilted his head and slid his gaze from the raven to Morgan. "You altered the wards to let her in without asking us."

"I didn't," Morgan promised. "Harper is here with the understanding that she's stuck in her human form until Kai approves of this."

Not *if*. Morgan knew exactly what was going to happen and Noah couldn't help the way his lip lifted in a silent snarl at that.

Why was she so fucking annoying?

He'd tell her to go bother someone else, but she'd brought him Harper, so Noah figured he'd give her another chance.

Something slammed into his back and Noah sighed when Lily's scent assaulted him.

"A raven?" she asked, peering over his shoulder to eye Harper. "Noah—!"

"Thank you for stating the obvious, Lily," Noah said, cutting her off.

Harper narrowed her eyes at the witch and his grin widened.

"Can we come in or what?" Morgan asked, setting a hand on her hip.

Why she always wore sweaters that were three sizes too big for her, Noah didn't understand, but he ignored her request and left that up to his Alpha to decide.

His eyes locked onto Harper's again, and he had no idea what to do about this new development when she hadn't told him anything other than the simple fact that she wasn't going to kill him.

If she was planning to kill the rest of the pack, he really didn't think Morgan would have brought her here.

Before he could stop himself, he was reaching for the fabric at her throat, but Harper caught his wrist before he could pull it down. Her sharp nails dug into his skin and Harper twisted, making him wince at the sudden flash of pain. "Are we starting the training now?"

"I don't understand," Shane said, pulling him away from Harper by the scruff of his neck. "I thought ravens never trained outsiders."

"I asked her nicely," Morgan purred, pushing past Noah and Shane.

Lily grabbed him when Shane finally let go, and dragged him into the kitchen, glancing over her shoulder as she opened the refrigerator. "What are the chances a raven would come here?"

Noah had the sudden realization that this green witch might know what Harper looked like. He took the half and half from her and tried to figure out how to ask what he needed to know.

"Are we sure this is a good idea?" he heard Jacob ask, muttering under his breath even though every shifter in the room could hear him.

"I trust Morgan," Shane replied, his voice tight despite his words. "Harper is unaligned apparently."

"Noah," Lily hissed, dragging him over to the coffee bar.

She started setting up the electric kettles and Sage was suddenly there, smiling shyly as she started a few pots of coffee.

"You would know the odds better than me, Lily." He poured the creamer into the porcelain pitcher and set it on a tray before going through their various sweeteners. "Out of curiosity, what are they?"

"Extremely low." Lily rolled her eyes and then sighed. "I wish Alexander were here."

"Your mate wishes the same." Noah arranged the packets of sweetener to look like flowers on a separate tray and then built a little tower of sugar cubes. "Is she the one you Saw?"

His entire body was vibrating with awareness.

It didn't matter that she was wearing those charms

to hide her scent and any sound she might make. They didn't cover up the thin bond between them that told him exactly where she was at all times.

At least he could physically see her.

"I don't know," Lily admitted, taking one of his sugar cubes and popping it into her mouth. "I only saw a raven, not what she looked like as a human."

Noah couldn't decide if he was relieved or not.

What the fuck was he supposed to do now?

Every atom and molecule that made up his entire being wanted to go to her, sink his teeth in her shoulder and neck over and over. The mark was probably gone, and he was slowly losing control as each second ticked by.

His scent could still linger on her skin, but no one would be able to smell it as long as she wore those charms.

God, she made him so fucking crazy.

Noah wasn't sure he could stay human if she kept acting like she didn't know him.

"You wanted a one hundred percent chance of winning, right?" Morgan asked Kai, somehow sounding like she was laughing at him.

This witch was such a creep.

"I did," Kai admitted. "I know you can see the future, but it's unusual that anyone can See it so clearly."

"Well, I could prove it, but I don't know if you'd like that," Morgan teased.

The sound of Morgan sitting down told him nothing about the raven. Noah glanced over his shoulder and found Harper studying the house, drifting around the wide-open space with the kind of grace only an assassin possessed, but she'd never been like that with him.

No, Harper was different when it was just the two of them, and it wasn't just the blank expression on her face.

This wasn't just a hunter – she was a killer.

Noah licked his lips and tried to convince himself that there was no good way to tell everyone she was his fucking mate, because she had no plans of keeping him.

His little raven stopped in front of Calvin and considered the lion. It was fascinating how such a strong, dominant Alpha didn't feel the need to stand up. He just looked up at her with a flash of gold and a raised eyebrow.

"I hope you're as nice to work with as your father was," Harper murmured, dropping her chin ever so slightly in a sign of what he might call respect. "You've always taken in the ones we couldn't."

Noah had no idea what they were talking about, but his chest was tight, and his wolf was thrashing against his human side, demanding they go over there and rest their chin on her shoulder to let the lion know she was *his*.

Not that it mattered. Kitty was their mate.

"Let me help," the human said, taking the tray of sweetener packets from the bar. She grinned up at him and Noah winced at just how bright and sharp her happiness smelled.

It assaulted him and he actually took a step back, needing space.

He needed to get the fuck out of here.

There were too many people, and too many scents. It was making it impossible to control his wolf.

"Hey." Suddenly Liam was there, his cold hand on the back of Noah's neck. His twin pulled him in, putting his body between Noah and the rest of them.

Liam pushed Noah's nose into his neck, forcing him to smell that familiar scent and only that. It cleared his head just a little as the sharp pine and icy river smell of his twin washed away everything else.

He closed his eyes and stood there, knowing Liam could feel his entire body shaking, but it was impossible to hide it anymore, not when *she* was here, in his fucking house, filling it with her scent without allowing him to drown in it.

Too many people, and none of them would understand.

Liam's grip on his neck tightened when the shaking only got worse. *Do we need to go on a run?*

His brother's thoughts brushed against his and Noah tried to retreat, but Liam held on too tight – both mentally and physically.

It felt like the coolest touch on the roiling, fever of his thoughts.

Noah didn't want Liam coming in contact with that. What if he poisoned his brother with his darkness? Liam didn't deserve any of this.

He was about to push him off, but another gentle wave of soothing thoughts washed over him. They weren't words, just concepts. Liam sent him pictures of the forest and their pack of feral and mundane wolves along with all the emotions that came with being free.

Liam still knew him better than anyone and Noah let himself lean into his brother, desperately needing that support when his kinky bitch of a mate was right there, and yet so far away.

Somehow, Liam finding his mate hadn't ruined their bond. It felt like a miracle.

What would happen if Harper decided she wanted to keep him? Would he still get to have this connection with his twin?

We should go on a run, Liam pressed, his thoughts tinged with worry. *You're too close to shifting right now.*

Shifting into a wolf wasn't the problem. The problem was how feral and needy his wolf got around Harper, and Liam could feel it. Noah couldn't say for sure that he wouldn't try to bite her again if he shifted, even with so many people watching.

His wolf didn't care about them, and neither did he.

"Tell me again why you're letting *this* wolf challenge an Alpha," Harper said, her tone sharp and challenging. "He can barely handle being around all these people."

Noah's eyes snapped open, and he found her watching him with that infuriatingly blank expression. Her brown eyes were still pretty, but they looked bored and lifeless.

Even without her emotions on, they'd never looked at him like that before.

His wolf couldn't handle it, and neither could he.

Liam cursed when he lost his grip and Noah shifted, snarling as he sprinted toward her.

He'd remind her that he wasn't some submissive, weak little thing that needed coddling. No, the only coddling he needed was from his twin and that was only to keep him from killing every fucking person in this room for looking at her.

Finally, her eyes filled with that spark when she grinned as he leapt over the couch, ignoring Zoe's sharp command that pulled at him, but it wasn't enticing enough to listen to.

Harper stood her ground, waiting for him as he charged.

"What a bad puppy," she murmured.

Noah stumbled at that soft, throaty tone. It reminded him what she sounded like when she moaned as he gave her pleasure.

"Sit," Harper commanded.

There was no pull to obey her. Noah usually felt *something* deep inside him when a dominant shifter tried to force him to obey with their will, but Harper was a raven. They didn't have the same submissive and dominant traits.

No, the only thing he felt was the desire to make her praise him.

His eyes narrowed, annoyed at her for being such a bitch. Why couldn't she just tell them who she really was? Why all these ridiculous games? And why the fuck was Morgan a part of them?

"I said *sit*, puppy," Harper purred, tapping his nose just like she had on the roof. "I want to look at you."

Oh.

Right, she had said she wanted to see his wolf form.

Noah found himself sitting like a damn dog, and his wolf was so pleased by her smile when he obeyed that his fucking tail started wagging.

It was humiliating.

"So pretty," she crooned, sliding a hand over his snout, and dragging her thumb across his sharpest teeth. "So deadly."

Okay, maybe it was worth the humiliation if she was going to talk to him like this.

No one in the room moved as they watched. Noah was pretty sure no one was even breathing except that damn witch who just smirked like she'd known this would happen.

"Do you want to bite me?" Harper asked, tilting her head as she slid her fingers through his fur.

Of course he wanted to bite her. Noah snapped at her arm to prove it, but she wrapped her fingers around his snout with her other hand, still petting him like he was an overgrown dog.

"Shall I train you first?" Harper asked, somehow strong enough to hold on even when he shook her.

Shit, she was way stronger than he'd thought.

Harper released him and went to sit in one of the empty armchairs. The way she looked at him sent a thrill through his entire body. Then she patted her thigh. "Come here, puppy."

Oh, Noah was going to make her pay for this later.

But he trotted across the living room to where she sat and plopped his head on her lap as hard as he could. Her sharp grin at the malicious compliance was exactly what he'd needed to see.

"Such a good boy," she whispered.

And just like that, those pretty brown eyes started to glow a gorgeous red that reminded him of the blood splattered across his room.

16

HARPER

She ignored everyone staring at them as she stroked Noah's fur, watching his aura finally settle as she soothed him. His ears were soft and fluffy, and his eyes were starting to close as he finally let himself relax.

His panic shouldn't have bothered her. Harper didn't feel anything after all. So why had she felt the sudden need to calm him down?

Watching him with his twin had been...disconcerting.

And now that woman, Zoe, was watching her like a hawk. Harper would be impressed how well she watched over both the twins if she wasn't so focused on calming Noah's aura.

They couldn't afford for him to go feral with so many dominant shifters in the room.

She understood why he'd started to lose it though. The scents clogging up this room were nauseating. Harper glanced at Morgan, and the witch nodded before digging in her purse.

So many auras were roiling, and the anxious scents made the muscles in her shoulders tighten. If they didn't calm down soon, she was going to kill them all just for a moment of peace.

There was a rumble in Noah's chest that was so low it was barely audible, but Harper could feel it in her bones. It wasn't a growl, but something close to a purr as he flopped against her legs and shoved his head farther onto her lap, so his nose was right against her stomach.

Harper almost took off her charms but ignored the pull to do one more thing to comfort him.

All of this was fucking annoying.

Her call with Valentina had been insightful, but Harper was still bothered about all of this. If her partner hadn't insisted on this cracked plan, she wouldn't have even bothered.

But for whatever reason, Valentina thought it was smart to get on this witch's good side and didn't see the harm in playing with a mate, especially one who would do anything for her.

Having someone on the ground to protect their backs was a plus in Valentina's opinion, and so was a witch on the West Coast who happened to be stronger than Faye.

It would cut hours off their flight time whenever they needed to buy more magic.

As unaligned ravens, it was always smart to make sure they had the kind of alliances that would help them stay alive without a flock or Enclave to shield them.

If they didn't pay off their contracts soon though, they'd need protection against the very same people who'd promised to protect ravens within the Enclave.

Harper wasn't a part of the Enclave anymore, and her life was theirs if she didn't pay for it.

A shadow swept over her, but Harper refused to look away from Noah. His twin's presence didn't bother her at all for some reason, and neither did his extremely dominant mate.

"Noah?" Liam asked, his tone careful but questioning.

Noah huffed dramatically and Harper found herself grinning again.

It was fucking irritating how many times this wolf had gotten her to do it when she'd decided to be as mean and as cold as she could for this little meeting.

"He's fine, Liam," Harper murmured, keeping her voice low and soothing. "Please make sure this meeting goes as quickly as possible. The scents in here are suffocating."

Liam's surprise and Zoe's amusement washed over her, and Harper felt the tension in her shoulders ease when Morgan *finally* lit those witchy candles that would clean the air of all the scents.

To her surprise, Liam sat down next to Noah with his back against her chair. Harper tensed again as she waited for Zoe to get all possessive, but the dominant wolf did no such thing.

Instead, she turned her attention to Kai. "I don't understand much about this new development, but I think it's a good idea."

Her aura told Harper it was because of these twins.

"I agree," Kai said slowly, watching Noah with a gleam in his eyes that told her he'd kill her the second she made a wrong move.

His Second, Shane, looked like she could knock him over with a feather. His shock and disbelief would have been insulting, but she remembered who he was from Noah's story.

Shane might figure it out before the others, but not before Liam.

Surprisingly, Harper didn't feel bothered by that, but she tweaked Noah's ear anyway. Stupid wolf had just stood there like an idiot.

He didn't want anyone knowing who she was, and Harper wanted to punish him for that, but it wasn't a good idea when he was ready to lose all sense of humanity.

Harper liked him feral, but if he never shifted back into his human form, she'd be annoyed. Ravens and wolves couldn't fuck in their animal forms.

"She will train this entire pack, for a price," Morgan explained, setting the first candle on the table next to her and Noah. "But she'll make sure you win the challenge, Alpha. As you know, a raven assassin has been trained from birth as a hatchling."

Her hands went still as Harper realized this witch knew more than she should for an outsider.

"They're trained to survive as soon as they can walk." Morgan set another candle next to the lions, smiling at them like they were best friends. Maybe they were if she'd grown up with leopards. "Did you know they spend a year on the ground as hatchlings without any interference from adults?"

Harper gripped Noah's fur tight as she resisted the urge to kill this witch again. She wasn't technically part of an eyrie any longer. None of this mattered to her, and she hadn't been the one to tell the witch all their secrets.

But she couldn't help but wonder who had.

"'The ground' means earth, essentially," Morgan said, setting two more candles down on the coffee table. "In Harper's Collective, which you might know better as a 'flock,' the hatchlings don't leave the eyrie until they're taken to the forest below them at four years old.

They leave them there for a whole year, to weed out the weak."

Remembering that year wasn't exactly bad, but Harper had forced herself to forget it for a reason.

"Before they drop them in the forest, they're taught to fish and hunt, how to build shelter," Morgan explained. "They are taught how to scavenge for edible plants and fruits, how to identify if abandoned or dead meat is safe to eat and how to prepare it, how to wield a knife, build a fire...all of them are capable by the time they've reached the age of four."

She should get up and slit her throat. Harper couldn't believe this witch knew so many details.

"They are constantly monitored thanks to the TIs – the training instructors, who watch over them. But they are never seen and never allowed to interfere." Morgan studied everyone in the room, probably reading their minds.

Harper hoped she could read hers, because if she said anything else, she'd snap, and Morgan would have brought it upon herself.

"But if a hatchling is starving, or about to die from exposure, they are taken back to the eyrie."

The weight of Morgan's gaze felt like a block of ice on her chest, and Harper stared into Noah's blue eyes as she tried to figure out what the fuck to *do*.

"Those that are removed early are still trained as assassins, as are all ravens, but they will never take a contract. They are taught to do any number of other things a Collective needs to function."

Harper pushed Noah's head off her lap and went to stand, but Liam's hand wrapped around her ankle faster than she could process and *squeezed.*

Watching the witch walk toward her was a test in patience the likes even her instructors hadn't tortured her with.

"Some TIs aren't fast enough," Morgan admitted, stopping right in front of Harper. "Are they?"

"One hatchling killing another is allowed," Harper agreed, her fingers twitching. She wanted to pull her blades out, but she was just one raven.

These shifters could tear her to pieces and Noah and Liam were touching her. If she slipped into the shadow realm, she'd drag them both with her and they'd get eaten by the creatures that lived there.

You watched her kill another, didn't you? Morgan's thought slithered into her mind and Harper locked down everything she didn't want the witch to see.

How did you know?

I can See anything I want to See, Morgan reminded her. *If it makes you feel better, Corbin and Emily needed to survive. If they'd died...us being here would be pointless.*

Strands of Fate felt like they were wrapping around her throat and choking her as she tried not to think about why Corbin and Emily were so important...

But not her.

I don't feel better, Harper thought, narrowing her eyes. *Because I don't feel anything at all.*

Really? Morgan tilted her head and smirked before sitting back down. *Are you sure that's true?*

What the fuck did *that* mean?

Something sharp pierced the skin of her finger and Harper hissed, seeing Noah pouting because she'd shoved him off of her.

Damn brute was too big for his own good. He was the size of a mundane bear and made this fucking room feel smaller than it already did.

"So, now you know what kind of experience she has. Harper will make sure you're well trained, Kai," Morgan said cheerily, like this was all normal and expected. "I've also noticed the wolves don't have territory alphas like the felines do. There's only one wolf on the Council, and they're from the East Coast."

"Because they have a deal with a demon," Calvin explained. "But having territory alphas has made sure to minimize the in-fighting among the felines, at least, in my opinion."

"Would you like for me to call the Alpha of the West Coast Pride?" Morgan asked as she pulled her phone out of her purse. "I'm sure he could give you some pointers, Kai. By the way, when is the challenge?"

"Like you don't know," Shane grumbled.

Tonight, if the witch was to be believed.

Harper clenched her teeth when Noah licked her finger, the ridiculously long tongue wrapping around until she wondered all sorts of things she shouldn't.

"I'm going to take a look around outside," Harper said, pulling her hand away from Noah. "Then we can get to work."

Stupid wolf.

This time, Liam released her.

Harper didn't let herself wonder what the other twin was picking up on. She just carefully made her way through the living room toward the front door, barely resisting the urge to slip into the shadow realm so she wouldn't have to feel all their eyes on her.

She had half a mind to call Valentina and tell her this was a mistake, and they needed to kill the witch after all.

"Noah," she heard Kai warn.

Pausing at the doorway, she glanced back to see the giant wolf following after her, just like he'd promised.

"It's fine." Harper couldn't help but admire how beautiful and dangerous he looked.

His fur was an interesting shade of white, but it was more grey-white which made her wonder what his twin looked like. Would they be identical as wolves too?

"After all, I don't expect you to let me wander around your property without an escort," she said, ignoring Shane's suspicious look as she waved Noah through the door first. "Enjoy your little chat."

Walking down those steps, she watched the wolf trot toward the trees off in the distance with every expectation that *she* would follow *him*.

Harper stopped at the bottom of the steps and looked up at the sky.

What was she supposed to do now?

Agreeing to this game with Morgan was one thing, but now there was a house full of wolves who knew what she'd had to survive just to earn her training. Then she'd had to survive that training to earn her place as a true assassin.

Why her, and why these wolves?

A short bark pulled her attention from the clouds in the sky and Noah wagged his tail once when he saw her looking at him, as if *he* were praising *her*.

Stupid wolf.

Harper felt a sharp grin spread over her face as she imagined all the ways she could punish him now that they were alone.

"Wanna play a game with me, wolfie?"

17

HARPER

She didn't wait for him to respond. Harper bent her knees and gave him a sharp grin, feeling the adrenaline start to flood her system. "Catch me if you can, puppy."

Before he could process, she took off, running as fast as she could past the barn that smelled like metal and engine oil. Harper didn't like how wide open the clearing was behind the house, but it was perfect for a full-out sprint.

Snow and ice dotted the marshy ground, but her enchanted boots gave her the traction she needed to use her full speed.

What these apex predators didn't know was that they may be the strongest, but many of the smaller shifters had gifts the apex predators didn't possess.

Ravens had many, but the strongest asset in her opinion was their speed and sight.

Noah was just as silent, but she could feel him behind her, pushing to catch up.

Harper glanced back and laughed when she saw him getting ready to launch himself at her again. Between one blink and the next, she'd slipped into the shadow realm.

The puppy missed, flying past her in confusion when she dodged. Now he couldn't see her *or* sense her.

Before he could panic, she exhaled and pulled his tail as she ran past him straight for the forest where she could sense mundane animals as well as what smelled like another wolf pack.

Those must be the feral wolves Noah had told her about.

When she reached the tree line, she slid into the shadow realm again and jumped, grabbing the lowest branch of the nearest tree and exited the veil. Harper whistled once and laughed when Noah whirled around, growling at her.

"You're pretty fast, for a wolf," she admitted.

Harper plopped her ass down on the branch and swung her legs, eyeing the wolf pacing below her. He wanted to climb up the tree and pull her down, but there was a chance he could actually hurt her, so instead, Noah anxiously watched as he started to wear a line in the muddy earth.

"Guess I win this round," she teased, stretching her arms over her head. "I didn't even have to shift, and I beat you. No wonder Morgan asked me to train you all."

Just like that, he was a naked human, glaring up at her.

Harper leaned forward, licking her lips as she studied his powerful body from head to toe.

"Why did you even agree to this?" Noah demanded, waving his hand back at the house. "Weren't you contracted to kill me?"

She swung her legs and shrugged. "I was. But now I'm not."

Noah glared up at her. "And why is that?"

"I'm pretty sure I told you why." Harper pushed on the branch with her hands, bringing her lower body up so she could perch just like she would in her raven form. "You proved to me you're more entertaining alive than dead."

He fumed as he looked up at her, chest heaving with his righteous anger.

But this anger was better than his panic. Harper watched him and his aura, making sure he didn't edge into that terror he had earlier.

"So now what?" Noah demanded, crossing his

arms over his chest, clearly comfortable in nothing but his own skin.

It was the first time she'd seen it in the daylight and his tattoos were so dark they glimmered under the weak spring sun. "I train you, and your Alpha."

"That's it?"

Harper narrowed her eyes. "Ask me what you really want to know."

His aura flared and Noah looked like he was going to climb up the tree naked and yank her down by her hair. Harper bared her teeth at him, silently daring him to do something that stupid and barbaric.

"You left me," Noah gritted out. He looked away from her, searching the trees so she wouldn't see the vulnerability in his eyes. "I had no way to reach you or know if you were coming back."

Harper dropped down from the branch and landed in a crouch before him, tilting her head as she stared up into those pretty blue eyes, and then she lowered her gaze to the semi-erect cock practically in her face.

"Didn't you say you'd follow me wherever I go?" she asked. Slowly, she stood as she wondered how he'd react if she just...sucked him off right here. "It's not my fault you're a bad hunter."

The look of disbelief Noah gave her made Harper laugh. This time she didn't resist and reached out, wrapping her hand around his cock.

Instantly, it was hard as a rock and Noah was panting, his entire body trembling for a reason other than panic now.

"I'm not a bad hunter," he gritted out. "You're covered in magic."

"Excuses," she whispered, stepping closer as she trailed her fingers over the ridiculous length of him. "You can sense me even when I'm wearing magic."

His eyes widened at that. "I suppose I could have used the mate bond."

She released him and studied the tattoos along one side of his chest and shoulder. They looked different in the daylight. "You didn't tell anyone about me."

"And what was I supposed to say?" Noah snapped, wrapping his hand around the nape of her neck. "That I found my mate, and oh, by the way, she wants to kill me and the whole fucking pack?"

Before she could respond to that, he yanked down her turtleneck and inspected her neck, like he'd tried to do earlier.

All his anger and rage and panic seemed to melt away when he saw the pink scar tissue across her throat. "How?"

She felt her eyelids slowly close at the sensation of his gentle fingertips trailing over the thick lines. It sent a pulse of desire and need straight down to her pussy and the damn thing clenched, demanding to be filled by the one filling her nose with his sweet pine and icy waterfall scent.

"I didn't want it to heal," she admitted, lifting her chin up to give him better access. "So, I slowed down my healing until I could rub black salt into it."

The flash of horror that went through his aura made her chuckle.

"Harper, that had to be excruciating." Noah pulled her closer, but she could tell how much he liked what he was seeing by the way his aura seemed to dance even with the darkest blue. In the sunlight, that dark sapphire glittered.

"Why didn't you tell them who I was when I showed up?" Harper pushed his hand off her throat and glared up at him. "I know you're smart enough to realize I wouldn't have come with that meddlesome witch if I'd planned to murder your entire pack."

Noah opened his mouth and then closed it as his surprise flickered, sweet and tart like lemon.

The silence between them stretched, and Harper tried to ignore the fact that he was naked, but she couldn't anymore, not when his huge pecs were right in her fucking face.

She reached out and tweaked his nipples, relishing in his sharp inhale.

"You pretended not to know me," Noah finally said, looking down to watch her cup his pecs like a man would. "Why are you so obsessed with my chest?"

"I didn't think they'd be squishy," she admitted, squeezing them like she had the first time she'd shown herself to him.

"Harper," Noah actually laughed and yanked her against him, so her face was pressed between those massive tiddies. "I love how weird you are."

She made a face but didn't argue with him. Harper was under no delusion that she was normal, by any means.

"Did you want me to tell them you're my mate?" Noah asked, his hand sliding up her neck to sink into her hair.

Did she?

"Not exactly."

Harper couldn't resist anymore, not when he was giving her the most mind-numbing scalp massage. She slid her hands up Noah's thick thighs and rubbed her nose against his chest.

"Explain it to me then?"

Noah's breath hitched when her thumbs dipped dangerously close to his package. The damn thing flexed against her, practically shoving itself between her legs.

"I just don't want anyone unmated to think they can touch you like they own you."

Her nails sank into his ass, and he pressed against her, his breath ruffling the hair on the top of her head.

"Olivia is one of my closest friends, and I can't

stand the humans. Everyone else is mated." Noah rubbed his chin against the top of her head, content to just stand like this.

Had seeing the mark on her neck really made that much of a difference? Noah seemed less feral and anxious. Harper wasn't sure what to think of that.

"Were you jealous?" he teased, resting his other hand on the small of her back to press her even closer.

Harper had to turn her head to the side or suffocate in his giant tiddies. She dug her nails into his ass harder but didn't try to pull away.

Was that witch right? Was she feeling...something?

"Your life is mine," she reminded him, deciding to leave it at that. "Don't forget it."

"Guess you'll have to stick around and remind me," Noah murmured, kissing the top of her head.

It was too cutesy for her, but Harper found herself letting him continue to hold her. Everything felt simpler when she could feel his heart beating against her cheek.

"Why are you so dead set on doing this challenge?" she demanded, biting his squishy pec in irritation. "I was going to kill your Alpha until I found out *you* are the idiot here, not him."

Noah's soft chuckle had her narrowing her eyes in irritation. This wasn't a laughing matter. Literally nothing about this was funny.

"If Kai loses, everything goes back to the way it was." Noah tightened his grip on her when she tried to push him away, so she bit him hard, sinking her canines into his flesh. "Keep that up if you want me to fuck you right here, and right now, little raven."

Blood filled her mouth, and she didn't let go when he refused to release her. Noah's soft groan was echoed by the rumble of his wolf in his chest and she suddenly felt achy and desperate.

"If I lose, Kai is still alive and can take down a wounded Alpha with no problem. Win-win." Noah hissed in a breath when she licked the bloody mark on his chest. "You don't have to like it, but you do have to admit I'm right."

Noah wasn't wrong if he only considered his pack along with his own abilities. This stupid fucking wolf wasn't planning to ask her for help, and he wasn't going to beg.

How disappointing.

"Get on your knees," she told him, taking a step back and kicking his knee at the same time. That put him off balance fast enough she gripped his shoulder and pushed. "Yes, just like this."

Noah looked up at her in surprise, still too damn big for his own good. Even on his knees, his head was taller than her chest.

Leaning down so her lips were right against his ear,

she watched as three others approached with disinterest. "Beg me to help you."

"I don't need your help, Harper." Noah wrapped his arms around her waist. He didn't bother to get up, even when her grip on his shoulder tightened painfully. "Cascade has no idea what I'm capable of."

"And you have no idea what *I'm* capable of." She gripped his hair and yanked back so he would see just how serious she was. "They are not as weak as you think they are. Let's say you do win, what's your exit strategy?"

Noah gave her this huge smile like he couldn't be happier. It even reached his eyes, but his aura darkened until all the sparkles were gone. "I'd be shocked if I lived long enough to have to worry about that."

"Such a *stupid* wolf," she hissed, absolutely furious.

"I told you, I've been courting death my whole life." Noah blinked up at her, surprise coloring his features. "Harper, you're crying."

That was impossible, there was no way she could cry, not without turning her emotions on.

Fat drops of water landed on Noah's cheeks, and she released him, stumbling backward as she reached for her face.

Her fingers came away wet.

"How is this happening?" More wetness rolled down her cheeks and neck. Harper tried to shift, but the magic guarding this land wrapped around her until it felt like it was going to squeeze her brain out through her ears.

"I told you," Morgan murmured, stepping through the trees. "But they aren't your emotions, Harper. They're Noah's."

18

HARPER

Was that even a thing? Could a mate's emotions transmit through the bond even if it hadn't been accepted? Harper was reeling from the shock of it all, and Noah wouldn't let her go.

It was too much between the scents that three new people brought, the physical contact, and the overwhelming sensation of *feeling* after years of feeling nothing at all.

Even though she'd been able to see Noah's aura, and all the aspects of his emotions, Harper hadn't known what it would be like to experience it all at once.

Underneath his quiet happiness that she was back and had implied she wanted him to come chase after her was the never-ending grief from what he'd experienced over the last decade.

Noah's depression was something he was used to dealing with, and he hid it well. But for Harper...his endless misery manifested in *her* body because the wolf refused to let others worry about him.

Why couldn't she stop crying?

Was it because he didn't plan to survive this mission he'd taken upon himself? Or was it the fact that he'd found his mate, and still didn't think life was worth living after giving his twin everything he'd promised him?

That wasn't even the worst of it, and she pushed Noah as hard as she could, not hearing anything over the roaring in her head.

Why wasn't she good enough?

Once more, her life didn't matter in the grand scheme of things. Harper was good, but not good enough.

Normally, she didn't give a flying fuck about the worth of her life as long as she wasn't bored, but now that these stupid feelings were suffocating her...she couldn't breathe under the weight of them all.

Cold hands gripped her face, and she pulled a blade, but Morgan was faster.

The witch dove into her head and created a barrier between Noah's emotions and her. It washed over Harper like a cup of hot honey and mint tea. For the first time in her life, she was grateful to have someone invading her privacy.

But...why now? Why hadn't his emotions affected her before this?

Because you accepted the bond, silly raven, Morgan murmured into her thoughts.

Now it felt like soothing chamomile, no sweetness to ruin the calming effect.

I'm pretty sure I'd remember something like that. Harper realized then that they were in the shadow realm, and everything was dark. *Did you bring me here?*

You disappeared and Noah nearly had a heart attack. It was irritating how amused the witch sounded. *So, I came to get you.*

Harper couldn't decide if she was grateful or not.

Morgan's laugh tinkled, even in her thoughts, and it was like cherry sorbet on her tongue, even in the soothing darkness of the shadow realm.

Accepting the bond doesn't have to be complicated, Morgan murmured, still holding that shield up between Harper and Noah. *Your little wolfie accepted it that first night, like the lovesick idiot he is. And you... you wanted him to stay with you instead of choosing to die for his pack.*

That's enough? Harper bared her teeth in annoyance, trying to find the lie in Morgan's eyes, but there wasn't one. Even her aura was a soothing purple instead of that nauseating pink. *How is that enough when I don't feel anything for him outside the affection I have for how entertaining he can be?*

Do you want him? Morgan tilted her head and brushed the hair back from Harper's face, completely unbothered and ready to wait forever for a response if need be based on the soothing spiral of her aura.

It was a simple question, but Harper searched those innocent-looking brown eyes and knew it couldn't possibly be that easy.

But it is. Morgan smiled and wiped the tears from Harper's cheeks. *You're a shifter. You don't have all the hang-ups that humans do. For you...you either want him, or you don't.*

And if he gets boring? Harper raised an eyebrow in question, refusing to believe what this witch was trying to tell her. *What happens if I never turn on my emotions?*

Do you really think Noah will care about your emotions? Morgan asked.

She glanced over the witch's shoulder and saw him pacing in his wolf form, his twin brother sitting obediently next to Zoe as he watched his twin with worried eyes.

No, she didn't think he'd care based on the pattern he'd established with her all the times they'd ever been together.

And if I get bored? she repeated, shifting her focus

back to the witch who Saw more than anyone ever should.

Either you kill him, or you turn your emotions on. Morgan shrugged like she didn't care, and for some reason, that made Harper uncomfortable.

What future had she Seen?

But until then, you want him. The witch shrugged again and gave Harper this quirky little half-smile that was the most natural, organic thing she'd ever seen her do.

The truth Morgan was showing her in the calmness of her thoughts and the simplicity of it all... this really didn't have to be complicated. If Harper wanted Noah, then that was just how things were.

Except, the consequences of that were this mate bond snapping into place and forcing her to *feel.* There was a reason she'd turned that shit off and kept it off even after leaving her Collective.

It's just like when you block me out, Morgan reassured. *You can shield yourself from his emotions like you do when you don't want me seeing that deeply inside your mind.*

That was only marginally reassuring.

Harper took a deep breath and tried to figure out what her next step was going to be.

The pull to leave the shadow realm and comfort her distraught wolf was stronger than she'd like –

enough that it was all she could focus on now that she had some room to think and catch her breath.

I don't want him challenging that Alpha. Harper refocused on the witch who was responsible for all of this.

There was no way Morgan could See so much... and do nothing. She'd kept quiet instead of telling the wolf pack about Harper and Valentina. There was a reason for that, and Harper knew it wasn't because she wanted to reunite Harper with her mate.

And it certainly wasn't this farce of training a wolf pack.

What if I told you he could challenge that Alpha, and live to tell the tale?

Harper bit her tongue instead of screaming, which would only bring the shadow creatures down on them like hungry little piranhas. *Why does it have to be* ***him?*** *Why not his Alpha? Kai doesn't want him doing this either. His life belongs to* ***me.***

Morgan slowly removed her hands from Harper's face and took a deep breath. Carefully letting it out, the witch suddenly looked exhausted – like she'd lifted a glamour.

There were dark circles under her eyes, and even though her skin looked undamaged, it looked...stressed. Morgan needed some electrolytes and sleep after eating a massive, protein-packed meal, but the witch still brimmed with the kind of power that could burn through a mortal body like it was nothing.

It has to be him because it has to be you. Morgan pulled the sleeves of her coat over her hands and then tucked them into the pockets. *It only takes two ravens to bring down an empire, right?*

Harper blinked and took a step back, not sure if she was hearing Morgan correctly. *It has to be me?*

Would you do anything in your power to make sure Kai lives? Morgan asked, shifting her body to reveal Noah circling around them, teeth bared in a terrifying snarl.

Somehow, he could sense her even in the shadow realm now.

You know I wouldn't. Harper watched her wolf hunt her just like she'd asked and wondered why she would make sure he lived no matter the cost.

Was it just to keep him around to entertain her another day? It had to be more than the sex, because otherwise she could go off and find someone just as proficient.

Valentina will do anything for you, Morgan admitted. *And you would do anything for her...and Noah. Maybe even Liam and Zoe by extension because you know your little wolfie couldn't live without his brother getting his happily ever after. Without you, this pack doesn't survive the war with Cascade.*

She rolled her eyes and crossed her arms over her chest. *You're exaggerating.*

Morgan gave her that quirky little half-smile again. *Why would I lie?*

To manipulate me into doing what you want, duh. Harper took a step to the side and watched the way Noah's eyes followed her. *Kai has a whole pack at his disposal. If Cascade doesn't want him as their Alpha, that's their right.*

A pack of baby wolves. Morgan watched as Harper moved again, her half-smile turning into a full one when Noah stopped circling them to stare at Harper's feet. *Cascade has too many fully grown and trained wolves. They'd rip him and Amelia to pieces before turning on the others. This pack will fall if we take that route.*

There was something the witch wasn't telling her, but Harper decided not to ask. If she knew what it was, she might just be contrary and do the opposite. She respected Fate and the Morrigan too much to mess around with shit like that.

Why this pack? Harper asked, taking a step closer to Noah.

The wolf stopped snarling.

It's already here, and it's better than Cascade. I can't get those wolves up north to listen to me, and that could end badly for everyone when hell is unleashed.

Morgan's eyes suddenly glowed pink and Harper

felt a shiver run down her spine. Whether that was literal or not, Harper didn't know, and didn't feel like asking.

If I choose this, what happens if I decide to leave? I don't want to live here. Harper crouched down and reached out, wondering if Noah would freak out if she touched him like this.

This pack will flourish and grow without you and Noah. It will continue to do so even if Liam and Zoe decide to go with you. It's too soon to tell which path they will take, but either way, the end result is the same.

Witches with the kind of power and Sight Morgan had...

If she wasn't a daughter of the Morrigan, she had to be a direct descendent of one of the other goddesses. It would be foolish to ignore a child of Fate.

And my contract? Valentina's?

I'll take care of it.

Harper tapped Noah's nose. *Clan witches and their money.*

He sneezed and she covered her mouth to keep from laughing out loud.

I'm not a recognized clan witch, but they did pay me a lot of money to make sure I never took my father's name. Morgan gripped Harper by the shoulder. *I'll pay off your contracts, and you'll be free. As long as you make sure Noah survives the challenge. Whatever you have to do, do it. I don't care how many people you have to kill.*

Harper grinned and stood. *Is there a bonus for every body I bring you?*

Witches could always use dead bodies.

Sell the bodies to whomever you want, I don't care. Morgan tightened her grip on Harper's shoulder, nails digging into her skin so hard it actually hurt. Harper was pleasantly surprised at how strong this witch was. *Do we have a deal?*

Why didn't you mention this when I met you at the café?

You hadn't accepted the bond.

Simple enough, and true. She knew Morgan wasn't lying to her.

Harper had charmed all the information out of her that she could possibly get, just like Valentina had asked.

We have a deal, Morgan.

Now she had a solution to two problems, but there was one last thing she needed.

Harper exhaled and released the shadows, dragging Morgan with her thanks to the witch's grip on her shoulder.

Noah didn't move, his nose pressing into her sternum. The moment the witch released her, all those foreign emotions washed over her again, but this time, Harper was ready.

Her own shield was just under the one Morgan had put up temporarily. Noah's emotions crashed through the space between them once Morgan's disappeared and washed over Harper's.

She wasn't as strong as the witch, but she'd been trained by various different Seers and night witches. The flavor of those emotions still made it through, but it no longer felt like she was drowning in it.

Could she speak to him through the mate bond? It couldn't be all that different from the thread Morgan had used to connect their minds. Harper searched for the bond between them and tugged on it.

Noah went completely still and stared at her in disbelief.

Shift for me, she whispered down the bond. *I need you to answer a question before I tell you something.*

Her wolfie blinked again and stumbled, suddenly a naked man. "I heard you," he stuttered. "Just like I hear Liam."

"Well, now we're finally getting somewhere," Zoe muttered, her arms crossed over her chest, and fingers tapping her arms. "What exactly is going on here?"

Harper ignored the woman and focused on Noah. "Tell me what it is you didn't tell your Alpha. What secret are you hiding?"

Noah stood straight, his entire body tense as he glared down at her. He was pissed and indignant.

"By the way, your brother's fur is a different color,"

Harper told him, smirking up at the angry puppy. "I didn't expect that."

Noah's jaw dropped and Liam wagged his tail, just like his twin did. Zoe muttered under her breath about how *ridiculous* they were, and Harper couldn't agree more.

"I can only ignore the Alpha command because of Liam," Noah whispered, glancing back at his twin. "If he's too far...I can't shove it off. Because of this...*gift*, Liam will never be able to protect himself. The command works on him, but not me. So...a catch-22 depending on what that command is."

The wry smile he gave her made her stomach clench and Harper didn't like the bitter taste of despair she could feel from him. It made her want to cry all over again, and that wasn't something she was ever going to do again.

"So, he has to come with us?" Harper asked, tilting her head as she considered the possibilities.

"I don't think so," Zoe snapped, her hand coming down on Liam's head too hard to be called a pat. "I can't protect them. I haven't shifted yet."

Annoying, but not impossible.

"What is it you wanted to tell me?" Noah asked, wiping a tear from her face.

Fuck, that was the worst part about all of this.

Harper huffed and glared up at him, annoyed he

had so many stupid emotions all the time. "Is that the only secret you're keeping about this weird ability?"

Noah's eyes narrowed. "Tell me, Harper. I didn't lie, not even by omission."

His irritation tasted familiar and soothing for some reason. She liked it.

Taking his face in her hands, she stood up on tiptoe and bit his bottom lip hard enough to bleed. The taste of sweet copper filled her mouth, and she grinned when Noah let out a little whimper.

"I accept the mate bond, Noah."

His shock and surprise almost overwhelmed his disbelief. "What did you say?"

"She accepts the mate bond," Morgan repeated impatiently. "Now, let's go before the rest of the pack wakes up. We're on borrowed time, people."

"What?"

Zoe asked the question the same time Harper did, and she spared the baby wolf a glance before focusing on the witch.

"What did you do?"

"They may be...asleep." Morgan shrugged, mischief twinkling in her eyes. "It's nothing you wouldn't have done, Harper."

A sleep draught? No, this was a night witch. With her power, she could simply command they sleep and there was nothing any of them could do about it.

Harper sighed. "We'll talk about this later. It's time for you to challenge an Alpha, Noah."

"I feel like I'm missing something," Liam said, suddenly just as naked and irritated as Noah.

It was disturbing how physically identical they were.

"Same," Zoe agreed, her cheeks pink as she tried not to make it obvious she was checking out her mate. "This raven is your mate, Noah?"

"That's what you're worried about?" Liam asked in disbelief. "Of course she's his mate. Noah hates ravens, and he practically climbed on her lap as a wolf instead of tearing her into tiny little pieces."

"I'm not a twin, Liam." Zoe huffed and looked at Harper. "He won't die?"

"He won't die," Morgan promised. "Now...if we could just..."

"If you could just escort them, I'll scout ahead," Harper told her. "Make a door or something, but I want you to go to Seattle first. It's a free city. I'll find you."

Thanks to the mate bond.

Annoying, yet useful.

"I'm going with you," Noah insisted, still looking shell-shocked.

"Can you fly, wolfie?" she teased, inspecting him from head to toe. "Did you grow a pair of wings and I somehow missed it?"

His glare made her laugh and she pulled him down to lick the blood from his lip.

"Tell you what, I'll meet you in Seattle. First one there buys dinner."

Morgan grinned and started pulling crystals out of her pockets. "Even you aren't faster than one of my doors."

"Perhaps." Harper offered her hand to the witch. "Now give me back my wings."

19

HARPER

It took less than ten minutes to fly from La Grande to Tieton, Washington. Ravens were slightly faster than modern planes, and the freedom to spread her wings and go wherever she wanted on a whim...

There was nothing quite like it.

A trilling call would tell Valentina she was there, and a second later Harper heard the response to her left. She banked and spotted her partner up in one of the tallest trees.

Valentina preferred to be as high as possible where no one could touch her.

Harper tugged on the bond between her and Noah, pleased to see he was already west in Seattle. If things went as planned, they'd be done with this shit before midnight and there was a hotel in Seattle she wanted to take her wolf to after everything was over.

The food was amazing as was the service and it was run by demons and ravens. If Morgan paid off her contract as quickly as she'd promised, Harper wouldn't have to avoid places like that anymore.

She landed on the branch next to Valentina and folded her wings against her back. They were quiet as Harper took a minute to study their surroundings.

Cascade may not have known she and Valentina were going to back out of their contract, but they had planned for it if the amount of wolves on patrol was any indication.

This was going to cause problems.

Harper made the noise to signal Valentina to follow her and then launched back into the sky. The other raven didn't hesitate as she took off, giving Harper space in the air, but still staying close enough they could protect each other.

It was easy to stay high enough in the sky to avoid the wolf patrols, but she wanted a closer look. Harper dove into the shadow realm and expertly avoided all the leaves and branches as she increased her speed.

They didn't have the time to waste if Morgan was right.

Valentina kept up effortlessly, even when they flew directly over the Cascade Range home base.

It was set up similarly to the Blue Mountain Pack homestead, but there were infinitely more homes, and they weren't nearly as nice as the brand-new, modern ones Kai had built.

These homes looked like they'd been built a hundred years ago and barely maintained despite the growth of the pack. It was easy to see the mark of time as more houses were built outside the Alpha's house.

Each decade was visible, and it created an aesthetic that made Harper nauseous.

It looked like they spent their pack money on other things...like magic. The wards surrounding the homes weren't as good as what Blue Mountain had, but Harper knew that it would cause problems if they didn't have Morgan on their side.

Even then...

Would Noah even be able to reach the Alpha to challenge him? The official declaration would be over the phone. It was probably happening right now if she were right.

Morgan was a terrifyingly powerful witch.

There were less than five on this continent who could build a door from nothing but their own power. A lot of demons couldn't even manage something that taxing, but night witches were special.

Just like blood witches.

There was a reason there were so few of them left, and a reason why blood witches had disappeared entirely.

No one liked the power they wielded, and how a

witch could challenge demons and gods like it was nothing. Too many forgot that witches were created by goddesses, and the strongest lines were direct descendants.

It was why ravens had served blood witches for so long, and now...they did what they could for the dark witches who were left.

Harper decided serving Morgan was better than nothing. It somehow felt right.

After all, it was the reason why ravens existed.

This job had settled into her soul like a missing puzzle piece, unlike any job they'd ever done before, and Harper had an uneasy feeling it was because of this witch and her visions.

Leading Valentina away from the Cascade pack's private land, she headed toward Seattle. They could talk there before joining the witch and the wolves.

She strategized on the way, knowing Valentina was doing the same even if she wasn't certain what the plan was.

No matter who came to challenge the Cascade Alpha, they would have died before they'd even reached him. If they'd managed to actually make it to the Alpha, they would have been too wounded to win.

They'd set up a gauntlet of sorts between all the patrolling wolves and the magic everywhere. It wasn't a fair challenge by any sense, especially when it wasn't held in a place that would be considered neutral.

Why had Blue Mountain agreed to this idiocy? Were they really that desperate? Or did Kai naively believe that everyone was as fair and kind as he was? A very good Alpha in times of peace, but a poor one in times of war.

Lucky for him, Morgan liked this pack the way it was.

Slipping out of the shadow realm, she dove for a park in Seattle where the mate bond felt strongest. It was like a beacon in a city of scents and auras. Focusing on it allowed Harper to ignore everything else, and for the first time, she felt grateful for such a strong bond, even if she was wary of what its strength meant.

Instead of going straight to Noah, she landed on top of an apartment building and shifted into her human form, rolling her shoulders back as information percolated and strategies were assessed and discarded depending on complexity and success rate.

"I take it you got the information?" Valentina asked, crossing her arms over her chest to watch Harper pace. "Why didn't you just call?"

"I didn't have the time. Things moved too quickly." She supposed she could have called before flying, but Harper didn't trust Morgan not to do something ridiculous and stupid to manipulate the future without informing her first.

At least she could trust Zoe to manage the witch and the twins for the most part.

Fuck the Alpha, those three were the first ones she was training.

"I accepted the mate bond." Harper stopped pacing and looked at her partner, wondering if she would be...bothered. "I won't let it affect our pairing."

"Congratulations." Despite the deadpan tone, Harper knew it was a genuine statement. "What's the plan?"

This was why Harper would never leave her partner. Valentina was the only person who understood her.

"My stupid, idiotic mate apparently has a special twin gift and wants to challenge the Alpha of Cascade and that witch thinks it's the only way for the Blue Mountain Pack to win." Harper crossed her arms over her chest and glared at nothing. "The night witch said she would pay off our contracts if we made sure he lived to tell the tale."

Valentina's eyes widened and not for the first time, Harper wondered if she had her emotions on or not. It was difficult to tell considering how much control Valentina possessed.

"Completely?"

"Yes, and on top of that, we're allowed to sell each body we drop and keep the profits." Harper couldn't help her feral grin as she imagined all the money wolf blood could get them, not to mention if they managed to skin the pelt from the body before it shifted back to human.

That was nothing when compared to the bones. How many necromancers would pay a pretty penny for shifter bones to make their runes out of?

Valentina looked impressed and she reached out to tug on one of Harper's orange curls. "I'm proud of you."

"For what?" Harper scoffed. "Doing my job?"

"For following through and then some. You charmed a very powerful witch and got our freedom out of it to boot. But that's not the only thing I'm proud of you for."

Harper eyed her partner warily. Valentina didn't usually speak so many words all together in such a short period of time. "What else could you possibly care about?"

"You accepted the mate bond. I didn't expect you to." Valentina tucked her hands in her pockets and eyed the park. The scent of wolf shifters and mercury was getting closer.

Why would Valentina care about that?

Harper stared at her partner and tried to figure out what that could possibly mean. "I thought you'd be annoyed."

"*You* are the one annoyed by everything." Valentina slid her gaze over to Harper and smirked. "A wolf is a powerful apex predator and a good ally to have. He also seems to calm some of your chaos, which I like."

"What about you?" Harper was so shocked she almost stuttered.

Valentina's eyes zeroed in on something – the twins no doubt. "I know you won't leave me, so I'm not worried about it. Wolves and ravens used to live together with our witches. It'll be nice to live that life again."

She followed Valentina's gaze and saw Morgan smiling at Liam and Noah as they argued about something, pushing each other, and generally being obnoxious, but both their auras were sparkling.

Even Zoe was happy as she walked beside the witch, eyes darting around as her dominant wolf felt the need to take charge and protect them all until Harper returned. It seemed like a trait she'd had before the bite, and the wolf had only made it stronger while giving her the tools to do something about the ones she cared about.

Harper wondered if the human would mesh well with them. Two born wolves with a special twin gift, two ravens trained from birth to be the world's deadliest assassins, and a night witch who could See the future better than anyone else on Earth.

"I want to serve that witch," Harper admitted,

taking a step closer to Valentina. "I don't think it would be boring."

"And if she's right and there are blood witches out there?"

"There are thousands of ravens." Harper took Valentina's hand and squeezed. "I think this is the right choice for us."

"If that's what you think, then I'll follow you wherever you want to go," Valentina murmured. "But first we need to make sure your pretty little mate survives."

"Both of them. He can't win if Liam doesn't live." Harper watched them stop at the agreed-upon meeting place. "All of them, actually. They'd make a good pack, don't you think?"

"Those four, plus us?" Valentina seemed skeptical, but she tilted her head and studied the witch casually chatting with the human. Every so often, Morgan would glance up at them and smirk. "I suppose I can see it. Strategy?"

"Let's put your sniper skills to the test," Harper murmured. "I'll draw them in, and you take them out."

"Inciting chaos? Why am I not surprised?" Valentina drawled. Her expression grew serious, and she turned to Harper. "I need to warn you, if it's your life or theirs, I'm choosing you."

Their oath was just as strong as the mate bond, if not stronger since they'd sworn it in blood.

"I can live with that." Harper squeezed Valentina's hand one last time. "Morgan will take care of the magic and Zoe will protect her from anything physical. I'll clear the way for the twins, and once the challenge has begun, we'll start cleaning up our exit route."

"You're not going to watch?"

"I already know he's going to win."

Harper whistled and all three wolves zeroed in on her and Valentina. Noah's aura practically exploded with fireworks when he found her, but his face was impassive and polite.

The other raven *giggled* – she actually fucking giggled. "He's so fucking gone for you, Harper. Look at those sparkles."

"He worships the ground I walk on, as he should," Harper reminded her. "At least he knows how to hide it."

"Doubt his twin doesn't know," Valentina whispered, nudging Harper with her elbow. "Do you see how the other one is grinning?"

She rolled her eyes. "Let's get them so the witch can make us a fucking door. And if I hear anything about sparkles over the comms, I'm going to stab you."

Valentina chuckled and adjusted the piece of pricey tech magic in her ear. "As always, I am your shadow and you are mine, Harper."

The oath they'd sworn to each other when they'd first became a faction settled into her blood and bones, and all the irritation washed away as she felt the reminder of what she was and always would be.

"I am your shield and your blade," Harper murmured. "I will not flee from battle."

Tonight, she would be creating a new faction, and they would no longer be just a pair.

Valentina grinned and pulled Harper to the edge of the roof. "Together we will serve the Morrigan's will and honor the blood."

"Every time you miss, you have to do ten shots of tequila," Harper reminded her.

Laughter echoed as Valentina jumped from the roof, pulling Harper along with her. They shifted into their raven forms at the same time and led the wolves to a safer location.

Harper would also be Noah's shield and his blade. He would survive this challenge, even if she had to kill every single wolf in that pack to ensure it.

20

NOAH

Valentina didn't look anything like what he'd expected. Though, if he thought about it for more than two seconds, Noah couldn't say what he'd thought she'd look like. Maybe someone just like Harper?

But Valentina was the opposite of his mate.

The other raven was much taller, and her hair was ridiculously long, but braided back. It was a normal color too, even if it was a striking shade of blonde. The raven wore a black baseball cap to hide the glimmer of the sun on her golden strands, and Noah wanted to ask her a million questions.

Harper had chosen her as a partner, and if he could just figure out why, he felt like he'd understand a lot more about his mate. But they didn't have time for that.

Morgan was drawing on a brick wall in an empty

alley with some weird-smelling crystal while Harper and Valentina watched the entrance and exit to the alley they were in.

Seeing her like this was strange, but also...not.

There was no playful attitude, and she reminded him of the feral wolves in the forest – always on alert and ready for anything.

He still couldn't believe she'd accepted the mate bond.

Noah honestly hadn't ever expected her to, not when she had no interest in turning her emotions on. That wasn't even something he'd wanted from her, and there was...something—*something* about the fact that she'd choose him as a mate without any of the emotions that were enhanced by the bond...

She hadn't even felt *his* emotions until she'd accepted it, and Noah still couldn't believe she'd picked him.

Why?

Not that he was complaining, but there were a million other people who could fuck her just as good or better, so what was it about him that she wanted to keep around?

It couldn't possibly be his sunny disposition.

"Let's go," Morgan ordered, waving Harper and Valentina forward.

The forest on the other side of the portal had a wicked cold breeze, but Harper didn't react even though he knew she felt the cold and didn't particularly like it.

She glanced back at him over her shoulder and Valentina smirked, staring up at the sky as she waited for her partner.

He liked the other raven. She balanced out Harper perfectly.

"Don't get ahead of us," Harper reminded him, checking her gear one last time. "And don't move forward until you hear the signal."

"He knows," Valentina murmured. "Stop fussing and trust me to do my job."

"It's him I don't trust," Harper muttered, pulling the mask over the lower half of her face. "Did you hear me, puppy?"

"I'll follow you, Harper." Even into hell.

Liam snickered and he heard Zoe smack him, but for the first time, Noah didn't mind. He didn't care who thought he was the most smitten, ridiculous creature to walk this Earth.

Harper had chosen him.

"You need to shift," Morgan instructed when Harper and Valentina walked through the portal.

His mate glanced back at him one last time, and Noah nodded. He could do this.

Then the two ravens...disappeared. Noah was never going to get used to that.

But now, he had the mate bond to tell him where she was, even when she was in that shadowy place.

Liam and he shifted at the same time, and Morgan muttered about their clothes before snapping her fingers to make those disappear too. Noah wanted whatever it was Harper had in situations like this, but that could wait.

He took off, following the tug of the mate bond through the forest as the sun started falling. Liam kept pace perfectly, the sound of their paws hitting the loamy soil would make anyone think there was only one of them.

A flicker of worry for the witch and the still-human wolf went through him, and Noah slowed down a fraction. Would they be okay?

Something ahead of him burst like a rotten melon, perfuming the air with magic.

They'd be fine.

Ahead of him was his mate, and occasionally he saw a flicker of her as she went from the ground to the air, and back again.

Howls filled the air, and his hackles raised.

Liam's shoulder pressed against his as they took the shortest, most direct route to the Alpha. The only reason they were able to do that was because of the two ravens, who were the most terrifying creatures Noah had ever laid his eyes on, and he'd seen some shit.

Harper pulled tails so swiftly, slipping in and out

of the shadow realm so quickly she looked like a phantom or a ghost. Her charms made her invisible to these wolves, and they turned and snarled, following the sight of her like some will o' the wisp.

Too many followed her, and he felt anxious until nothing but a brief disturbance of air above them warned him.

All five bodies dropped in quick succession.

Noah leapt over them, catching the burning smell of silver and blood – enchanted bullets went through the brain and heart.

Just like that, he realized how easy it would have been for these two to take out his pack. Noah felt incredibly fucking lucky they were on his side.

Harper had *chosen* him.

Then Liam started smelling like anxiety and nerves. Noah could tell his twin was distracted by his mate, but there was nothing that could touch her with Morgan there, ripping apart magical traps all around them.

A wolf came from the side, and he dodged, shoving Liam out of the way. Before he could engage, Harper was suddenly there, appearing out of nowhere with that silver blade she'd teased him with the other night.

The way she grabbed the wolf by the nape of the neck, pinning him to the ground with nothing but her sheer will and strength. That blade sliced long and deep, slitting his throat in less than a second – Noah had never seen anything more arousing.

"*Move*," Harper ordered, eyes glowing that sinful ruby.

Noah didn't hesitate. He put on a burst of speed, running as fast as he could through the last of the forest. Something popped and sizzled as he leapt over the wards guarding the property line, and he heard the chirping signal from Valentina.

He and Liam wove through the endless houses toward the one in the very center where the Alpha was waiting. Shadows chased him, and he felt the mate bond between him and Harper stretch as she stayed behind.

The sun was setting faster, and he refused to lose by something as stupid as being late. Noah snarled as wolves started exiting their homes, following them forward.

He was still pissed the Alpha had refused to accept his challenge unless it was here. Morgan had insisted it would be fine, but he should have insisted on neutral territory.

It made him uncomfortable to have just Liam there instead of the whole pack, but he trusted Morgan, Harper, and Zoe to keep his twin alive if the worst was going to happen.

There was a large clearing in front of the Alpha's house that looked like children played there regularly, but at the moment, it was lined with wolves in their human forms.

All of their eyes were glowing silver.

Noah slowed down to a trot, getting ahead of his brother as he tried to ignore the raven he could feel just behind his heart.

Blake Scavage opened the door to his house and stepped out onto the porch with a smirk on his face. The Cascade Alpha had a good ten to fifteen years on Noah, but that didn't mean anything in the grand scheme of things.

There was no doubt who was the more desperate wolf, and Noah had come here with nothing to lose.

"I was expecting Kai, not you," Blake said, his deep, booming voice laced with the power of an Alpha who had a strong pack supporting him.

Liam trembled beside him with the force of it, but there was no command paired with that power, thank fuck.

Shifting, he placed a hand on the back of Liam's neck, just like he'd done for Noah earlier. "And yet, you accepted my challenge."

"To be fair," Blake drawled, eyeing Noah from head to toe. "I didn't think a submissive wolf would make it this far. And unscathed as well. I'm impressed."

Noah's lip lifted in disgust. All ten years they'd suffered in the Blue Mountain Pack, this fucker had done nothing. He'd even occasionally worked with the Alphas that had destroyed his life, willing to look the other way.

And now...he'd waited until they'd started to recover before attempting a petty takeover. Why hadn't he done it when the pack had been at its weakest? Why had he waited until they had hope again?

There was no way Noah was going to let him ruin this.

"Are you scared to lose?" Noah asked, tilting his head like he'd seen Harper do as he raised an eyebrow.

That smirk on Blake's face dropped and the animosity he felt from the enemy wolves in the front yard was suffocating. This had to be fast, but not too fast. Noah had to make sure Harper was close enough when he won or these wolves would tear Liam apart, and then him until they were nothing more than blood and shards of bones in the frozen mud.

"Afraid to lose against a submissive wolf?" Blake scoffed and shook his head. "I'm going to do the right thing and give you one more chance to back out. Let your Alpha handle this like a good little puppy."

A deep growl escaped him. "Only one person gets to call me that." Noah stepped into the circle of enemy wolves and waved his hand to indicate he was waiting.

Blake snarled and ripped his shirt off as he came down the steps of his ancient porch. It was a miracle the damn thing didn't collapse under his weight. Kicking off his boots, the Alpha's eyes started glowing as his body prepared for the shift.

He definitely had to be fast. This fucker was huge, like most true Alphas were. Despite his age and the salt and pepper hair, Blake was built like a fucking freight train.

Noah had to end this in one strike, or he might not survive.

"This is a mistake you won't be able to come back from," Blake told him as he unbuckled his pants. "You can't win against me. It's impossible."

Liam huffed a wolf's laugh behind him, and Noah smirked. Just a few more seconds – he had to buy Harper a little more time.

"Then I guess this won't take very long, will it?" Noah asked, rolling his shoulders back to get ready for another shift.

"My Third will give the call," Blake said, stepping out of his pants. He tossed them to the side and one of the massive wolves behind him shifted into his wolf form. "That okay with you?"

"Go for it." Noah cracked his neck and then shifted into his wolf form, feeling Liam behind him.

I got your back, Liam told him. *Don't worry about me. Just make it quick.*

He had no intention of dragging this out.

Blake shifted and the size of his wolf was goddamn

intimidating no matter how much Noah believed he could win without issue. His fur was a grey and tan with nasty teeth that could probably tear his insides out with just one good pull.

The last traces of the sunlight disappeared and the Cascade Third howled long and loud, warning everyone that a challenge for rank was starting.

As he expected, the Alpha didn't wait. He threw his dominance at Noah with all his strength and all the power of his pack.

Kneel, the Alpha demanded.

It washed over him like a tidal wave and Noah dove for the Alpha, ignoring Liam's whimper of pain as he was forced to the ground. The shock on Blake's face wasn't enough to make him feel better about his twin, and Noah sank his teeth into his neck.

The fur was thick though, as were the Alpha's muscles. Noah gripped hard and slammed Blake to the ground, and then shook.

It was enough to make the Alpha lose his focus, and the command disintegrated. Liam's pain was no longer suffocating Noah and he grinned as strength and adrenaline filled him.

Now to finish the kill.

He'd taken too long though. Blake struck with his back feet, claws digging into Noah's ribs as he danced away.

It hurt like a bitch, but nothing broke. He struck

again, aiming for the exact same spot on Blake's neck as before. Another command washed over him, but Noah ignored it and tore his teeth from the neck.

Blood splattered on the ground this time and the Alpha snarled, dazed, but still conscious.

This wasn't going to end well, and Harper was going to be pissed.

Noah sank his teeth in again before the wound could heal, using all his weight and strength to slam Blake into the ground again. This time he chewed, taking the kicks to the ribs.

More blood fell and steam rose in the cold, dusky air.

It was time to finish this before he fucking died. Noah pulled back and bit the Alpha over and over, tearing his throat out again and again until there was so much blood soaking the ground it turned into slick mud and the two of them started sliding around.

The silence was more ominous than any amount of snarling and growling would be.

No one had expected this.

There'd always been a chance that Kai would come and win considering how strong he was. But Noah was a submissive, and he was winning thanks to the element of surprise.

He shifted out of his wolf form, tasting blood. The Alpha stumbled as he tried to stand, and Noah ignored the wounds all over his body as he dropped his knee on

Blake's ribs, feeling a flare of satisfaction when they cracked.

"You should have left my pack alone," he growled, wrapping his arms around the Alpha's neck, ignoring the pitiful snap of those dangerous teeth.

Before the healing could kick in too much, he snapped the Alpha's neck and then planted his foot on the spine and tore the head from the shoulders.

The wolf's head hung from his hand, dripping blood and nerves as his chest heaved.

Noah had won, but now he had to survive that victory.

He'd done exactly what he'd said he could do, and now...now he had to make sure Liam survived, even if it cost him his life. Harper would be fine, wouldn't she?

Weirdly, no one came for him, and the waiting was making him restless.

Pain suddenly radiated through his leg, but it wasn't his – no, it was his twin's.

Noah whipped around and saw the enemy wolves had already made their move. Liam tore someone's ear off as he fought against way too many of them to survive alone. Noah dropped the head and dove into the fray, shifting into his wolf form midair.

That's when the rest of the wolves finally attacked.

He might not be able to hold them off for long enough. Noah felt panic slice through him as he ripped out someone's throat at the same time that Liam yelped.

Harper, please hurry. We need you.

Pressing his side against Liam's, Noah fought back, and prayed his mate would get there in time.

21

HARPER

There was so much pain, but not all of it wasn't hers.

Harper, please...

She ignored the curse she'd stepped on that was digging into her ribs and gave the signal to Valentina to take care of the rest and flew as fast as she could to the location where she could feel the other end of the bond.

No matter how much she'd been annoyed about this whole mate thing, Harper couldn't stand the way it felt when it started fading.

Noah was dying.

That wasn't something she was going to allow. His life was hers after all, and so was his death. He'd promised it to her, and some stupid fucking wolf wasn't going to take it from her.

Slipping into the shadow realm was too easy. Finding the pack of snarling idiots was simple enough, and she shifted as she exhaled, leaving the shadows for the cold night.

Blade in one hand and gun in the other, she made the enchanted bullets count, digging the blade into hearts and throats as she whirled through the madness to where she could see a pair of grey-white and white-grey wolves fighting for their lives.

They were both severely injured but holding their own and Harper had never seen anything as beautiful and vicious as Noah in that moment.

Then she became a flurry of death and retribution.

Every time a wolf got too close, she slipped into the shadows and dragged them into the glittering veil with her, and then left them there after sinking her blade into their side.

Soon, she wouldn't be able to use the veil now that she'd basically left a feast in her general location. Harper pulled as many wolves into the shadow realm as she could before she heard the unearthly screeches that always had the hair on the back of her neck rising with her body's animalistic response to a dangerous predator.

Survival instincts told her to *move*, and she exhaled right as claws of darkness reached for her.

Harper twisted and fired two shots into a wolf's head before finally reaching the twins. Noah was barely standing, but he kept using his body as a shield for Liam.

Shooting the rest of the wolves surrounding them, Harper released the magazine and grabbed the last one from her belt.

Those blue eyes found hers and Noah's relief nearly had her knees giving out. Harper braced herself against the wave of his emotions, and the pain she could feel through the bond that was making him slower.

His healing didn't seem to be working at the moment either, not when he kept getting reinjured.

Noise warned her and Harper fired as three more tried to leap toward them.

Then she inspected Liam.

Her mouth tightened as she realized just how thin the rope that these two were hanging on was. One more attack, and that rope would snap.

More wolves surrounded them, but they were hesitating now that she was there. The pile of bodies making a barrier around them didn't hurt either and Harper picked her way over them to the twins.

Just how many fucking wolves were in this pack?

Liam was the first to collapse, and she knelt beside him, slipping the pack off her back as she eyed the other wolves waiting for an opening.

Then Noah was kneeling beside her as a human, covered in blood. Most of it wasn't his, but too much was. "I'm sorry. I should have dragged it out a little longer. Harper, tell me you can save him."

She clenched her jaw and yanked a healing potion out of her pack. "Pour this down his throat."

Noah coughed then and she focused on him and the wet sound that came out of his mouth. Blood flecked his lips and there was a flicker under her heart – something that almost felt like panic.

"Shit," Noah muttered, struggling to take the cork out of the vial. "Harper..."

She caught the vial, and yanked out the cork with her teeth, dropping her gun to grip Liam's chin.

Fuck, fuck, *fuck,* this was bad. She had maybe three seconds.

The soft sound of paws on soil warned her and Harper poured the healing potion down his throat. Closing his mouth, she massaged his throat as she reached for the second vial.

Two more seconds.

"Harper..." Noah collapsed, and she pursed her lips, biting off the cork for the second vial as she scooped up her gun. "I don't think...I don't think I want to die."

Something squeezed her heart so hard tears fell onto his face. It could have been the curse, but she had a feeling it was something else.

"You're not going to die," she promised, staring into his eyes as she poured that liquid into his mouth. "I didn't give you permission to leave me, Noah. So, hold on."

Harper leaned down, mentally counting the milliseconds in her head as she kissed him, making sure he drank the potion.

"Valentina told me it only takes two ravens to bring down an empire," she whispered, kissing him one last time as she brought up her gun. Harper closed her eyes and fired, using nothing but the sound to guide her. "So, a single raven should be enough for one little pack, don't you think?"

Not waiting for an answer, she pushed off him and spun, firing as her training kicked in.

There was no way these wolves could compete with her when she had a long-range weapon, but they could overwhelm her and start tearing little pieces off of her just as they'd done to Noah and Liam.

Throwing her knife, she knew it sank into someone's eye by the sharp yelp, and grabbed the second gun from her pack, swiveling around with both arms up.

There'd been more magical traps in the forest than she'd expected, and that had slowed them down to have to wait for Morgan. Then there was the issue that most of the wolves had been spread too far apart to really get a lot of them to cluster together.

She and Valentina had ended up adjusting for their second strategy which allowed them to separate, and then reconnect at the most opportune times. Harper would always bring more wolves, taking them down as she moved, and Valentina would shoot at anything that wasn't her, the twins, or the human and the witch.

Bodies littered the forest, and the curse she'd stepped on was still lodged in her side, but it wasn't slowing her down, at least not yet. Harper was used to working in impossible conditions, but eventually the tightening on her ribs would crack them and crush her.

She was going to trust the dark witch to See what was going on and do whatever was needed to make sure Harper followed through on their deal. Letting these idiots kill her was not in Morgan's best interest, fortunately.

Teeth closed around one wrist, but she aimed and shot the wolf in the stomach before shooting straight up into the jaw.

Shit, she needed to reload.

Harper spun, stepping back to get closer to her pack where more ammunition was, but she was too far away.

Click, click.

Fuck.

Anyone who hadn't attacked made their move the second they heard that sound, and Harper braced herself for the hand-to-hand combat. It wasn't going to end well if Morgan didn't hurry the fuck up.

Her hand reached back, unconsciously searching for Noah who was just behind her, and she crouched, baring her teeth as she took inventory of the knives on her person.

Five wolves, with three more behind them. She could take out three without too much issue and take some damage from the remaining two before killing them. That would give her the time to throw two knives, and then...

One head exploded and then four more in quick succession.

Harper grinned, throwing two knives at the others behind the wolves popping like balloons. She spun and reached for another knife, throwing it at the same time their head popped.

"Show-off," she muttered, grinning as she waved.

The pain was making it difficult to locate Valentina, but if she was within fifty miles of her location, then Morgan would be close.

Harper stumbled as her ribs finally cracked. Hopefully, the witch was *super* close.

Noah caught her before she fell, already looking a thousand times better thanks to the healing potion. "What's wrong? You're hurt, but I can't smell it."

All the curse would allow were tiny little panting breaths, but she fought against it to pull the charms off her neck, wincing when the titanium chain got caught on her hair.

Noah's pupils dilated the second her scent hit the air, and she patted his face to reassure him. "Liam?"

"I'm fine." Liam groaned and she felt him move before his face suddenly popped over her. "I smell magic."

The nasty curse had popped her protection charms and Harper wasn't looking forward to the bill when she got them replaced.

"What do I do?" Noah demanded, shaking her when her breathing became little more than tiny inhale. "Harper, you're not allowed to die either."

"We have another problem," Liam muttered, his eyes shifting to something she couldn't see, but could sense. "We should take her and run."

That was the best option, but Harper didn't have the oxygen to tell them as her ribs snapped again, pressing into her lungs.

"She's in so much pain." Noah held her face in his hands and searched her eyes desperately. "You think I can take some of it?"

"You're not a fox," Liam hissed, his eyes darting around as the snarling wolves got closer. "And she's not your twin."

Such a weird thing, twins.

Harper smiled up at Noah, unbothered by the situation. Either Morgan would save her, or she'd die. It wasn't all that complicated. She'd done her job and saved the twins.

Valentina would be free to do whatever she wanted without her Collective and the Enclave looming over her.

The only thing she wasn't too pleased with was how panicked and violent Noah's aura was getting. If she died...

If I die...she reached for him, wiping some of the blood off his face. *I'll wait for you in hell.*

"If you die, I'll bring you back to life," Noah growled, his eyes so bright they were nearly blinding. "Just so I can kill you myself."

She'd laugh if she could.

"Harper," Valentina's breathless voice reached her even through the brain fog, and she slid into her, running a tattooed hand over Harper's body. "You fucking idiot. Why didn't you say anything earlier?"

Because Noah had called for her.

"Do you have anything for magic?" Liam asked when Noah snarled at the raven, pulling Harper into his arms.

The pain had eased somewhat, and Harper had a feeling her precious idiot was taking it through the mate bond. Why he wanted to suffer, she didn't know, but Harper blocked off the mate bond just in case.

He didn't need to feel her death.

"Calm down, Noah," Valentina snapped. "Let go of her or she'll die."

Shockingly, her mate listened, and her partner

pulled something out of her pack. It wasn't going to remove the curse, but it should help if it was what Harper thought it was.

She laughed when the luck charm hit her skin and she could finally take a deep breath – just one. But it would give her the time she needed to wait for Morgan.

They'd trained to hold their breath for a long time after all.

"So stupid," Valentina hissed, her eyes red. "I'm going to kill every wolf in this pack."

"Not the children, or the innocents," Liam argued. "But otherwise, feel free."

Just as Valentina summoned her pistols, a chorus of howls filled the night sky.

"It's Kai and Shane," Liam said in shock. "They're here?"

She laughed again, taking in another breath through sheer will alone despite the pain. Morgan had always planned to bring them, if she was right.

Taking over this new pack wouldn't be easy, and two submissives, two ravens, a witch, and a dominant wolf who wanted nothing to do with anyone outside the twins wouldn't have been able to control a bunch of wolves who needed an Alpha to hold them together.

A door opened and Morgan stepped out, her hands already reaching for Harper with that pink fire lighting up her eyes and casting a strange glow around them. It mixed with Valentina's ruby and her partner made room for the witch.

"You did a good job," Morgan murmured, kneeling to rest one hand on Harper's forehead, and the other on her chest. "You did exactly what we needed you to do, and then held on. Your stubborn personality saved your life, Harper."

Noah held one hand and Liam took the other. Valentina stood and hovered over the witch, her guns up as she guarded their backs. Zoe was suddenly there too, administering first aid to Liam first, but the healing potion had done its job.

"Her ribs are cracked and they're piercing her lungs." Morgan had sweat dotting her forehead. "I can heal her, but I'm going to need to borrow some strength from the two of you, so don't let go."

Both twins nodded and Harper couldn't believe she'd left the only support system she'd ever known and somehow...

Somehow she'd found a better one – one that was more suited to her personality and tastes. But wolves and a witch? Who would have thought it would end up like this?

Her eyes closed as strength from the twins was pulled through her fingertips. She could feel that strength being directed towards her chest while Morgan ripped apart the curse with half a thought.

This witch had probably known. She'd probably

known long before Harper had ever left her Collective. Meeting Valentina during one of the Enclave meetings had felt like Fate, and so had this contract.

A contract she never would have been able to take if she'd stayed with Corbin and Emily.

Had Morgan Seen everything from birth? Had she watched Harper's life, and the twins? Had she been a teenager, wishing she could help, but not having the strength or training to?

Well, if Harper survived, she was going to make sure this nosy-ass witch had the help she needed to make sure other people like Harper and Valentina survived whatever horror they couldn't deal with alone.

"Morgan," Shane snarled, making Harper's eyes pop open at the furious tone. He shifted as he ran towards them. "We *trusted* you."

Zoe put her body between the witch and Shane at the same time Valentina aimed one of her guns at him.

"I wouldn't if I were you," Valentina warned. "I will choose Harper every time, no matter what the twins feel about you."

Morgan ignored everything as she focused, sweat dripping down her face as she stitched Harper's lungs back together before working on her ribs.

It was excruciating – far more painful than when they'd been shattered. Harper gritted her teeth, panting through the agony as sweat poured down her face and back.

"All those dead bodies? These two ravens did all that," Zoe told him, the dominance laced into her voice was just as powerful as the Second's, if not more. "Noah beat the Alpha, and the ravens kept them alive long enough for you to get here. So, do your fucking job and make sure the Cascade pack is subdued. Morgan did this for you and Blue Mountain."

Shane eyed them and pursed his lips. Then he sighed heavily and ran a hand through his dark hair. "I can't believe you guys pulled it off."

Valentina didn't lower the gun even when Zoe set her hand on Liam's bare shoulder. The pain on his face eased and Harper wished the witch would hurry the fuck up.

Morgan giggled, her eyes glowing so bright it lit up the night sky. "Think you can handle it, Harper? It's going to hurt worse than anything you could ever imagine if I speed up."

"Just get it over with," she gritted out, taking in a deep breath to brace against the vicious pain.

Finally, Valentina shifted her focus and dropped the gun, giving Harper a nod. She'd make sure the twins and the witch were protected.

"Do it."

Searing pain ripped through her chest like Morgan was using red-hot hell-forged iron to put her back together. The witch was right. It was the most excruciating thing she'd ever experienced, even as a raven.

But Noah shared that pain with her, and the last thing she saw was his blue eyes staring into her soul when her body put her out of her misery.

22

NOAH

Holding Harper in his arms while she slept was the only thing keeping him sane as Kai and Shane talked over his head with Zoe bristling at every look they threw at him.

Liam was back in his wolf form and Valentina was helping Morgan, who looked pale but surprisingly alert for someone who'd just put his mate back together after destroying the curse that was killing her, plus whatever she'd done to get them all there.

And if what he was hearing was right, Valentina and Harper had taken out nearly eighty percent of the Cascade pack and he just...couldn't believe the way things had turned out.

His original plan had been to keep Liam as far away as possible and take down the Alpha, or die trying, but this...

His mate had destroyed the pack that had tried to decimate his hope as well as Liam and Zoe's future.

Now, the Blue Mountain Pack could truly rebuild without having to constantly worry about the enemy on their borders or look over their shoulder thanks to the old Alpha's mistakes.

Not when they'd made their strength very clear tonight, even if that strength had been bought and paid for by his mate.

Was Morgan sure she was okay? Ravens had quick healing, and she'd just been fixed up by a powerful witch with healing abilities.

It seemed there wasn't much that Morgan couldn't do.

"She's fine," Morgan assured, leaning onto Valentina and letting the raven take her weight. "It shouldn't take long. She's too stubborn to be kept down for long."

Noah buried his face in her hair and breathed in the clean scent of the night sky, mango, and the mate bond.

Someone crouched beside him, and he did his best to ignore Kai, but now that everything was over, he was feeling just a little bit guilty. Morgan had knocked out the entire pack out so Noah could directly disobey his Alpha.

"Noah." Kai's voice didn't have an ounce of his

dominance in it, but it was still a tone he couldn't ignore. "You were right."

That got him to look up, and Noah couldn't believe what he'd heard.

Kai smiled and gently set a hand on his back, between his shoulders. It was reassuring enough Noah felt the tension in his neck and back loosen. "I'm still upset that you and Liam got hurt in the process, but you two handled it well."

He wasn't going to burst Kai's bubble by explaining all this was because of Morgan and Harper, so Noah kept his mouth shut and nodded.

"She's your mate." It was a statement, and Noah realized that the entire pack could smell her now that the charms were off. "Why didn't you tell us?"

He glanced at Liam, and his twin pretended like he couldn't hear their conversation as he paced in a circle around them, keeping watch now that he was better than new thanks to Morgan and Harper.

"I wasn't sure if she'd want me," Noah admitted, deciding to be honest instead of hiding all his truths in ridiculous commentary that always distracted everyone from the fact that he hadn't actually answered their question. "But she accepted the mate bond before we came here, even without her emotions on."

Kai's hand was warm, and he let out a soothing rumble that was almost like a purr. It was one of the things that dominants and Alphas did that Noah had no power to resist.

The sound instantly made him feel safe and relaxed, but he held Harper closer, nervous about wherever this conversation was heading.

"I'm sure she can see how special you are regardless," Kai murmured, leaning in to get a better look at Harper. "She's pretty amazing, Noah. I'm happy for you."

"You're not pissed off?" Noah raised an eyebrow and studied his Alpha, skeptical that everything could be so easily forgiven considering the body count. "If the Council finds out about the number of bodies she dropped..."

"The Council will find themselves no longer living if they decide to look into this," Valentina cut in, her deadpan tone somehow making her sound more threatening, not less.

"Yes, well..." Kai trailed off as he studied Valentina, and Noah realized then that he had no idea who she was.

"That's Harper's partner," he explained, wishing she would just wake up already so he could hear her snark at him about how cold it was. "They're both unaligned."

"I'm aligned with Harper," Valentina corrected, handing Morgan a potion.

The witch's extended silence was making him edgy.

"Calvin and Caleb will be here shortly," Morgan announced, smiling slightly as she snuggled into Valentina. "They'll help with the takeover and the clean-up. I also called Samuel Erikson before we left. He's going to help you set up a territory Alpha for the wolves in the Pacific Northwest. It'll take a few months to get things to a new normal, but I'll be here to help. So will the ravens."

Both of his eyebrows rose at that, but Noah didn't question Morgan, not when she'd most likely already Seen it.

But why would Harper stay?

Obviously, Valentina would stay, because Harper was going to, but Noah couldn't figure out why she'd stay here. He'd fully planned on having to leave the pack and follow her around, just like he'd promised.

Morgan's smile widened. "All they'll ask is for your pack to return the favor when they need it. Caleb's pride is dying. He needs more allies whether he wants them or not. I refuse to let my home die because he's a stubborn asshole."

Noah choked as he tried to hide his bark of laughter, but Liam was laughing too, and even Zoe was grinning as she finished tying off the last of Morgan's bandages.

"Alphas are annoying like that," Valentina agreed,

dead serious as she scooped Morgan up into her arms like the witch weighed nothing. "I'm taking her to Seattle to recover. Harper too. The puppy is welcome if he wants to join."

Okay, maybe two people were allowed to call him that.

Noah stood, holding Harper against his chest to make sure she didn't get cold. "I'm definitely joining."

There was no way he was going to let Valentina take his mate away from him, not when she technically had seniority over who chooses where the raven in his arms was going to go.

"Of course," Kai agreed, wrapping a comforting arm around Noah's shoulders. "Take some time with your mate but stay in touch. I'm still responsible for your safety."

No matter how he felt about things, Noah knew Kai was a good Alpha who would make sure things were handled. He'd bring Cascade under his care and do with them what he'd done with Blue Mountain.

"I'm going with them," Zoe announced, crossing her arms over her chest. "Liam and I would like a break to celebrate our mate bond."

"Just be back before the next full moon," Kai told them, ruffling Noah's hair. "And if you're going to walk around in your human skin, maybe put some clothes on."

Oh, right. He was naked. Noah looked down and saw he was covered in blood too.

"You're not going to wait for Caleb, Morgan?" Shane asked, holding out his arms for Harper.

Noah hesitated, and then decided to let him take her. There was no one he trusted more than his brother, Shane, and Alexander to take care of what was precious to him.

Well, and Valentina, he supposed, but she currently had her arms full of a sleepy witch.

"He'll still be here tomorrow. I'll come back after I've regained some of my magic," Morgan said, dropping her head on Valentina's shoulder and closing her eyes. "Make sure to put all the bodies in one of the empty houses. They belong to Harper and Valentina."

He paused, and then decided he wasn't going to ask about that.

Noah pulled on a pair of jeans that Amelia had brought and the sweater that Bonnie had waiting for him. "Are we driving?"

"I can't carry a witch and fly," Valentina drawled, giving him a look that practically demanded he use his brain. "Can you?"

He sighed and just knew both these ravens were going to drive him up the wall with their attitudes. Liam huffed another laugh and Noah grinned right back at his twin.

Why do you act like you can't stand the idea of that?

Liam teased, brushing past Zoe. *Every time you look at her, you've got hearts in your eyes, dude.*

Yeah, there was no denying that.

Maybe I wasn't expecting a package deal.

Universe probably did that on purpose. Liam pushed Zoe toward Valentina as Noah yanked on a pair of boots. *Considering we're kind of a package deal.*

His heart squeezed and Noah really hoped that would be true even if he left the pack.

But...maybe it was time he and Liam figured out how to have separate lives. And there was nothing that said they couldn't join up again at some other point.

Noah took his little raven back from Shane and gave him an awkward thanks...it was weird considering all the drama they'd had with ravens over the years, but the last year plus a mate had been really good for the Second.

There was no sign of his OCD despite the chaos going on around them or even the weird control issues he had even with Bonnie around two ravens and a witch.

It seemed like they'd all grown, and the trauma would never be forgotten, but it was fading. Kai had given them a safe environment, and Noah had made sure their new home wouldn't get destroyed.

Now...now they had the freedom to really invest in whatever future they wanted without fear that it was going to be taken away. Noah had a mate who somehow fit him perfectly, and he knew that if this was possible for him...

Then he had no doubt Olivia would find something that was exactly what she needed, whether she knew what that was or not. He had faith things would work out, and in the meantime, he and Liam would be there to support her just like they'd always been.

Harper would just have to deal with it.

Let's go. Liam pushed Noah this time and herded him toward Valentina and Zoe. *We'll come back tomorrow.*

"I have no plans to come back tomorrow," Noah muttered, adjusting his grip on Harper. "But feel free to do whatever you want."

There's no way you can fuck that long. Liam snorted as he walked beside Noah.

"Wanna bet?"

Actually, I do.

Noah shook his head, but he was smiling – for real this time.

"Don't forget to call," Shane called out – always such a mother hen. "I'll worry if you don't."

"Be safe. Have fun," Kai called after them. "And don't worry about us. We'll take care of this."

"We won't," Valentina said, stopping to look around. "Where's the car?"

Morgan pointed with her eyes still closed and

Noah felt his stomach dip again when he realized it was one of Cascade's. It was unlocked and there were keys in the center console.

Creepy, but useful.

"Kai is a good Alpha," Morgan murmured as she crawled into the front seat. It was amusing to watch her let Valentina buckle her in. "But this was the only way to keep the Blue Mountain Pack alive. I'm sorry, you guys, I wish there'd been another way."

Liam hopped into the back seat when Zoe opened the door for him, and the human eyed the SUV skeptically. "Why is that?" she asked.

"Harper doesn't love Kai."

Noah snorted and shoved his twin out of the way so he could climb in, settling his sleeping mate on his lap. "Harper doesn't love me either."

"Love doesn't always look the same on everyone," Valentina told him, staring into his fucking soul like she could read his thoughts just as well as Morgan. "She wouldn't have accepted the mate bond if she didn't care about you."

He was speechless as he stared at the raven with her ruby red eyes that never really faded into her human color. "I thought either you had emotions on or you didn't. So, how does that work?"

Valentina shrugged and closed Morgan's door before walking around the SUV to the driver's side.

Zoe managed to squeeze inside too, and Liam rested his head on her lap with a little happy, goofy sigh.

"Do you love to eat?" Valentina asked as she started up the engine.

What the fuck was he supposed to say to that?

"I do," Morgan volunteered.

"Me too," Zoe agreed.

"I mean...I guess?"

"But whether you loved to eat or not, you couldn't survive without food." Valentina adjusted the rearview mirror so Noah could see those glowing eyes. "Harper can't live without you, but more importantly, she chooses not to. That's all you really need to know."

Noah felt his jaw drop, and he thought that maybe he understood why Harper had chosen Valentina as her partner.

Liam wagged his tail and smacked him upside the head with it as he readjusted.

"If you hit me with that thing again, I'm cutting it off," Harper grumbled, pressing her face into Noah's chest.

Relief washed over him. Noah dropped his head back against the seat and closed his eyes. He held her tight and ignored her squeaking.

"Your tits are suffocating me," Harper complained, pinching one of his nipples.

There was that sass he couldn't live without. "You

say that like it's not one of your favorite things about me."

"Gross," Zoe muttered as she scratched behind Liam's ears.

Harper sat up straight and nearly knocked Noah out with the force of her head colliding with his chin. "They have the exact same body! You can't say *gross* when Liam's tits are just as big."

Zoe's cheeks got pink, and Liam's tongue lolled in amusement.

She's got a point. Liam caught Noah's eyes and practically snickered. *But Zoe would rather die than admit it.*

"It's not my favorite thing about him," Zoe argued, refusing to look anywhere but out the window as Valentina navigated the SUV down the dirt road.

"Fine." Harper slumped back down and wrapped her arms around Noah's neck, making him speechless once more. "Their dick is definitely the best part. I'll give you that."

Liam snorted and Noah sighed, wondering if they were going to have to compare every single fucking thing for these two.

Zoe didn't have anything to say to that though, and Noah couldn't believe she'd chosen not to have the last word. Her cheeks were super red, and he looked away, hoping she hadn't seen his grin.

Humans were super cute sometimes.

"No more dick talk," Morgan whined. "You're going to make me puke."

"Agreed. Now tell me where I'm going." Valentina glanced back at him in the rearview mirror.

Was she really expecting him to answer?

Harper replied for him, just as he assumed he would for the rest of his life. "Take us to the Hotel Sorrento."

23

EPILOGUE

NOAH

Sliding under the covers, Noah gently pulled Harpers knees apart and buried his face between her legs, licking slowly as she slept. It wouldn't take long for the sensation to wake her up if the last twenty-fours were any indication, but Noah knew she was exhausted.

Between the never-ending fuck-fest, and all the healing she'd done, it was a miracle she could still get wet, but his tongue flooded with the taste of her – sweet and tart mango.

She also smelled like the mate bond, and something he might even call indulgent affection.

Swirling his tongue, he pulled back the skin so he could tease that swollen bud, grinning when she unconsciously lifted her hips to meet his mouth.

They'd taken a nap after they'd arrived at the Hotel

Sorrento. Valentina had ordered food and then demanded everyone shower before sending them off to their assigned rooms.

Noah had been so jacked with adrenaline and stress that he really hadn't been expecting to fall asleep, but Harper had let him hold her and the blankets were soft and cool, helping him regulate his unnaturally high body temperature.

Nothing screamed 'hotel owned by shifters' quite like the thoughtful additions for his kind which included a massive Alaskan king-sized bed, as well as a shower and bathtub big enough to fit his wolf form and then some.

There'd been a million things he'd wanted to ask her, or talk about, but she'd fallen asleep so fast there hadn't really been an opportunity. Then he'd fallen asleep moments after her, tired from the fight, the stress, and all the healing.

Another long lick and she sighed contentedly in her sleep.

It took her another couple of minutes to get close, and then suddenly her thighs squeezed his head like she was trying to crush him. Noah slid two fingers inside and sucked her clit in her mouth, relishing in the curses she muttered under her breath paired with her soft moans.

"Noah, what do you think you're doing?" Fingers threaded through his hair, but she didn't shove him away. Harper brought him even closer, grinding against him until she was shaking and shivering a few seconds later.

He'd never get tired of hearing his name on her lips as she whispered it over and over while he ate her out through the orgasm.

Pushing up, he positioned himself between her legs, rubbing the head of his cock against her sensitive clit, admiring the way she writhed beneath him, eyes glowing that gorgeous ruby red.

"You know it's going to be impossible to get rid of me now, don't you?" he asked, pushing forward with his hips so he slid inside just an inch, making her clench around him. "You accepted the mate bond and claimed me. There's no way I'm going to let you get bored and fly off without me."

Harper wrapped her legs around his waist and pulled him closer, making him sink into her. Noah felt his eyes closed as the sensation washed through him, making him tremble as he held back.

Every time he sheathed himself inside of her, it was a fight to keep from exploding inside that soft warmth, but this time, he didn't feel like he'd go feral at any second, not when he could still see his brutal claiming mark.

Noah traced the ravaged skin with the tips of his fingers and almost wished he'd been gentler, but

Harper liked it the way it was and that was enough for him.

"What's the plan now?" he asked, stroking in and out of her lazily. "How long will I get to have this?"

Harper's eyebrows raised and she looked irritated. "You're asking that now? While you're inside of me?"

He grinned and gently placed one of her legs over his shoulder, kissing her calf as he kept pace. "At least I know you can't run away and avoid the question like this."

She huffed, but shockingly didn't argue with him. Harper gripped the sheets and lifted her hips. Watching her eyes roll back into her head when he hit that spot she liked so much made his canines ache.

Running his sharp teeth along her calf, he watched her as he kept thrusting, feeling the tightness in his lower back that warned him he was too close to keep fucking around.

Noah sank his teeth into her calf, leaving a new claiming mark, one much smaller and daintier than the other one. He licked it clean and then yanked her forward, pounding into her hard enough her tits bounced in time with each movement.

He gasped when the orgasm hit hard and fast. Noah exploded and pressed down on her clit, rubbing it in time with each spurt and she came again – so lovely and pretty with her flushed cheeks and bouncing tits.

"So delicious," he murmured, licking the mark on her calf. "So gorgeous. What am I going to do with you, hm?"

"Fuck me again?" Harper rolled into him when he collapsed beside her on the bed. "You better be taking some kind of contraception, or I'll gut you."

Noah wrapped his arms around her and pulled her close. "I'm not, but I will be as soon as Morgan is all better."

Ruby red eyes glared up at him. "Lucky for you I'm on contraception."

"Definitely lucky." Whatever she wanted was fine with him. "So, what's the plan Harper?"

"I train your stupid pack, starting with you and your brother. Once Zoe has shifted I'll train her too. Valentina will help while your Alpha figures out how to manage both packs."

Rubbing his chin on the top of her head, he wrinkled his nose when her curls tickled. "You'll be staying with us?"

"Mhm."

It sounded like she was going to fall asleep again.

"What happens after that?" He slid a hand down her spine, and over the curve of her ass.

Harper sighed and rubbed her face in his chest which made him laugh. She was so fucking cute. "I don't know. I don't want to live with your pack."

"Okay." He dipped his fingers toward her back

entrance and licked his lips when her breathing hitched. "I'm not good at much, but I'll do whatever I can to contribute."

She arched into him when he spread the slickness between her legs around her back entrance. "Don't lie to me. Tell me exactly what you're good at, other than sex."

He grinned when his dick flexed against her stomach. Noah pressed a single fingertip to her asshole and circled it slowly. "I'm a glorified mechanic and an artist. I can fix pretty much anything on a car if it comes down to it, but I like painting more. And I'm really good at it."

Harper pushed back into his finger and Noah leaned down to kiss her, stealing what he could while she was distracted.

But this time, she sighed into him, kissing him back so sweetly that his brain fizzled into nothing. Her heat encased the tip of his finger and Noah groaned when his dick flexed so hard he nearly came on the spot.

"I know you're good at killing," Harper whispered breathlessly as she squirmed, trying to get more of his finger inside her. "And I have a feeling you're good at the housewife shit too."

He laughed at that. "I am, but honestly I thought that's something Valentina would like to do."

Breathy whimpers came from his mate as he pushed his finger in farther until he was two knuckles in. That was more than enough to make him forget everything else, especially when she licked his bottom lip before slipping her tongue into his mouth.

"Valentina hates doing that shit." Harper pushed back more, clenching around his finger like crazy. "Noah, stop teasing me."

"Am I teasing you?" He nipped her jaw, inhaling the mate bond, and something sweet that reminded him of honey mixed with lust. "Do you want more?"

"I want everything," she confessed, kissing him hard.

Noah tasted desperation and the mate bond between them was strong and sure, sending down warmth and affection through that bond.

"I'll be a good wife, if that's what you want," he murmured, pressing his finger all the way inside her. Harper moaned into his mouth, and he pulled out, gently stretching her as he went. "Is there anything else you want?"

"To edge you until you're begging," she hissed, biting his bottom lip when he left her empty.

"Next time," he promised, carefully pressing two fingers to her entrance. "I'll take care of you for the rest of my life, however you want me to do that."

It was unreal how easily both fingers slid inside thanks to being covered in their juices. Her heat squeezed him, and Noah nearly went feral at the idea of replacing his fingers with his dick.

"Promise?" Harper asked, grinding against his dick.

Jesus, he might not make it long enough to take her ass before she drove him crazy.

"I promise." Noah carefully pulled his fingers out and pressed a kiss to her forehead. "As long as you promise not to leave me."

Harper didn't hesitate. She turned around and pushed her ass against his dick. "As long as you don't care that I might never turn my emotions on, and you follow me..."

The head of his cock slid through her folds and Noah used his cum and her slickness to cover his dick before pressing it against her ass.

"If you're worried about my brother, don't be." He pushed inside of her, gritting his teeth as she clenched around him so tightly it was nearly impossible to keep moving.

Little thrusts in and out helped him slowly burrow inside her, but it was driving him fucking mad and Noah bit down on his claiming mark, trying not to lose control and hurt her.

"You'll leave your precious twin for me?" Harper reached back and wrapped her hand around the nape of his neck. She used that to press back into him, forcing him to get even deeper inside her,

"He has Zoe now. Liam's a big boy, he can take care of himself." Noah gripped her hip and pushed against her until he was seated to the hilt. "Do you like this?"

"Mhm." Harper wriggled against him, grinding back on his dick, and it was almost enough to make him bust. Her fingers on the back of his neck dug in so hard they were bound to leave bruises. "Are you going to just lay here, or are you going to fuck me already?"

Noah slid his hand down her hip until he found her clit. "I just want you to know, I really don't care if you decide to never turn your emotions on," he confessed, rubbing little circles into her clit. He needed her to come, because if he started really moving, he was going to fucking lose it way too fast. "You can't live without me, just like we are now. That's more than enough."

Her little whimpers as she chased her orgasm were precious and she pulsed around him in time with each breath, making his brain focus on nothing but the pleasure that he could give her – that he could *take* from her.

"Promise you'll stay with me," he murmured, feeling just how close she was. He kept his pace slow and even as he rocked against her, torturing her just like she'd tortured him. "And I'll never ask you for anything more."

Harper worked herself on his cock, giving him that friction he needed so badly, but he couldn't afford to lose it yet.

Just like that, he had her on her stomach, and his teeth in her neck like she was a naughty pup, but his fingers never stopped moving and she went wild beneath him.

"Promise me, and I'll give you exactly what you want, sweet little raven. I'll fuck you so good, you'll want to do it again and again and again..."

God, she was so fucking perfect. Noah would never forget the noises she made as he kept her on the edge of an orgasm, seated fully in her ass while her entire body clenched around him.

"I promise," she cried out, trying to reach down to force his hand to move faster—*harder*. "I promise I won't leave you, stupid fucking asshole."

He huffed a laugh into her neck and pulled back, taking her with him.

Noah sank two fingers inside her and used the heel of his hand to force her to come, shivering when she screamed and nearly snapped his dick off with the convulsions.

Before the orgasm could end, he shoved her down and gripped her hips, fucking her just like she wanted him to. It didn't take long once she started whispering *yes, yes,* ***please*** *yes*, under her breath over and over again.

The force of the orgasm almost hurt this time and he winced, feeling the sweat dripping down his back as he tried to catch his breath. Noah brushed the hair away from the back of her neck and kissed her there, enjoying the sweet taste.

"Just don't get disappointed when I remind you of your duties," Harper mumbled into the bed. "You have to be a good partner, Noah. Like Valentina."

"Does she fuck you this good?" he asked, leaning back until they were on their sides again.

Noah was content to stay like this for the rest of the day, dick deep inside her, sleepy and warm, with the window cracked open to let in that chilly breeze. Harper was perfect, and she'd made sure he lived to see another day.

There was nothing more he could ask for.

"She's good at fucking, but she doesn't have a dick," Harper admitted, pulling his arm around her middle tighter. "We've only had sex a few times though, when we needed to relieve some stress and couldn't find other willing partners."

The thought of them together had him hard all over again.

"Don't get excited, puppy," Harper said with a little laugh. "She's *very* picky about anything with a cock."

"I like her," he confessed into her hair, breathing the mate bond in until it settled in his bones once more. "She's funny."

Harper barked out a laugh – but it was almost too harsh to be amusement. "I suppose she is."

"Morgan implied you two were going to be here for a few months." Sleep was calling his name, but Noah wanted a little more time with her. He wanted to understand.

Other than training them...why would they want to stay?

"Did I ever tell you that ravens were created by a witch goddess?"

"No, you haven't." He pulled the blankets up around them, making a mental note to call the front desk for fresh sheets when they woke up again.

"We ravens were created to serve blood witches, but they're extinct now," Harper admitted, lacing her fingers through his. "Though Morgan says they're not."

Fascinating. Noah didn't think he'd ever heard of a blood witch, even if he knew what blood magic was.

"Either way, it's in our nature to serve the dark witches, and something in my gut is telling me that I should help Morgan with whatever madness she's planning."

Harper hummed then, her heart slowing as she got sleepy.

"A harbinger for the witch with true Sight?" Noah decided he liked the idea of that. "I'm just a wolf. How can I help?"

"Ravens and wolves used to live in packs together," she murmured, kissing his knuckles. "I want to make a pack with you, Noah."

His heart stopped beating for a moment as he tried to imagine what that would look like—what that *meant*.

Harper, the raven without emotions, wanted to make a pack with him.

"Does that pack include Liam and Zoe?" he asked, watching as the sun started to rise.

This time, he didn't have to worry about her disappearing at dawn. Harper had promised to stay.

"If they want. I like Zoe. She's smart and exactly the right kind of bossy." Harper kissed his knuckles again and then her breathing evened out, telling him she'd fallen asleep.

A pack of his very own...

Noah suddenly felt like the insufferable and excruciating weight he'd been carrying over the last ten years had disappeared, leaving him weightless and free.

"I want to make a pack with you, too Harper." Noah kissed the claiming mark on her neck and smiled.

Valentina was right. Love didn't always look the same on everyone, but on Harper it was fucking breathtaking.

For the first time in over a decade, Noah was looking forward to the future.

Thank you for coming on this journey with me. This is the end of the original pack's stories within the Blue

Mountain Pack. There may be standalones added later on, but I'm not sure when or if that will happen.

As for Olivia, she's going to get a crossover story, and I have plans for her, but there is no link for that book yet. I'm not sure when it will get done. Hopefully in the next year.

If you want to know more about ravens within my paranormal world, you can read the story about the witch Morgan told Harper about - the one who will change the opinions of witches about shifters. It is complete.

Something Wicked

If you're feeling more like a story with a raven as the main character, you can meet Emily, also mention in this book in her own series starting with:

A Bandit's Prequel

Thank you again and don't forget to check out my other books if you're feeling like some more paranormal <3 Emma

WANT FREE STORIES?

EMMA DEAN

If you subscribe to my newsletter you can get these shorts free on Bookfunnel!

A Bandit's Prequel

(Short steamy reverse harem shifter story.)

If you're subbed you also get the chapters of the first book before release!

A Steamy Xmas Short Story

(A reverse harem paranormal story about a witch and her three human boyfriends.)

Royal Guard of Draga

(Novella prequel for a Game of Thrones in space, or Dragonriders of Pern slow burn story that turns into a reverse harem, this is also steamy and just the beginning.)

OTHER BOOKS

Emma Dean

MAFIA ROMANCE

A Syndicate of Blood and Chaos

Born in Blood

Blood and Chaos

Ruled by Blood

PARANORMAL ROMANCE*

Blue Mountain Wolf Pack (M/F Wolf Shifters)

Alpha Wolf

Broken Wolf

Wolf Moon

Wolf Curse

Wolf Bite

Wolf Claim

Chaos of Foxes Series (Reverse Harem/RH)

For Fox Sake

All Foxed Up

What the Fox

Chaos of Foxes Boxset

This is Bandit Territory Series (Reverse Harem/RH)

A Bandit's Prequel

To Catch a Bandit

Make Out Like Bandits

Queen of the Bandits (2022 release)

University of Morgana Academy Series (Slow Burn Reverse Harem/RH)

Something Wicked

Wicked Games

No Rest for the Wicked

A Wicked Raven

Wicked Blood

As Wicked As They Come

Wicked Little Things

The Wicked Will Rise

Wicked Queen

The Infernal Royals Series (M/F UF Romance)

The Devil's Huntress

Whiskey and Hellfire

The Mark of Cain

Standalones (Reverse Harem/RH)

Spotted Her First

Vaudeville Runaway

SPACE FANTASY

The Draga Court Series (Polyam/RH)

Princess of Draga

Crown of Draga

Jasmine of Draga

Heir of Draga

Queen of Draga

Fate of Draga

Prequel Novella – Royal Guard of Draga*

Christmas Epilogue Novella - Winter Solstice in Draga

*Can be read as a standalone before or after Princess of Draga, but in the timeline takes place before Princess.

*All paranormal stories are in the same universe - the Council of Paranormals.

Want updates on when the books are released and my progress with them?

Sign up for my newsletter @ emmadeanromance.com

COUNCIL OF PARANORMALS TIMELINE

Council of Paranormals Timeline

A Devil's Huntress

Alpha Wolf
Broken Wolf

Whiskey and Hellfire

Wolf Moon

Vaudeville Runaway

Wolf Curse
Wolf Bite
Wolf Claim

Spotted Her First

For Fox Sake
All Foxed Up
What the Fox

A Bandit's Prequel
To Catch a Bandit
Make Out Like Bandits

Something Wicked
Wicked Games
No Rest for the Wicked
A Wicked Raven
Wicked Blood
As Wicked As They Come
Wicked Little Things
The Wicked Will Rise
Wicked Queen

ABOUT THE AUTHOR

EMMA DEAN

Emma Dean is the author of Draga Court and the Council of Paranormals. Juggling work, life, higher education, and a rambunctious toddler leaves little room for much else, but when she gets the chance she dives into a good book or Lego set.

Follow her on Social Media or

www.emmadeanromance.com

facebook.com/emmadeanromance

bookbub.com/authors/emma-dean

amazon.com/Emma-Dean/e/B073Z3XZ4X

ACKNOWLEDGMENTS

- Cover Art by We Got You Covered
- Content Editing by It's Your Story
- Proofreading by Mystique Editing

Made in United States
Orlando, FL
02 November 2025

71761997R00184